ECSTATIC CAHOOTS

ECSTATIC CAHOOTS

Fifty Short Stories

STUART DYBEK

Farrar, Straus and Giroux

New York

Farrar, Straus and Giroux
18 West 18th Street, New York 10011

Grateful acknowledgment is made for permission
to reprint the following material:
"Psalms (Although The Lord Be High Above)," © Don Heffington / Ceiling
Boy Music (ASCAP), courtesy Wixen Music Publishing, Inc.
"It's Raining" by Guillaume Apollinaire, translated by Roger Shattuck,
from *Selected Writings*, copyright © 1971 by Roger Shattuck,
courtesy of New Directions Publishing Corp.

Library of Congress Cataloging-in-Publication Data
Dybek, Stuart, 1942–
    [Short stories. Selections]
    Ecstatic Cahoots : Fifty Short Stories / Stuart Dybek. — First edition.
        pages   cm
    ISBN 978-0-374-28050-5 (paperback)
    I. Title.

PS3554.Y3 A6 2014
813'.54—dc23

2013033912

Designed by Jonathan D. Lippincott

Farrar, Straus and Giroux books may be purchased for educational, business,
or promotional use. For information on bulk purchases, please contact the
Macmillan Corporate and Premium Sales Department at 1-800-221-7945,
extension 5442, or write to specialmarkets@macmillan.com.

www.fsgbooks.com
www.twitter.com/fsgbooks • www.facebook.com/fsgbooks

1   3   5   7   9   10   8   6   4   2

For Tracy, with thanks

"They're a rotten crowd," I shouted across the lawn. "You're worth the whole damn bunch put together."

. . . First he nodded politely, and then his face broke into that radiant and understanding smile, as if we'd been in ecstatic cahoots.　　　—F. Scott Fitzgerald, *The Great Gatsby*

It's raining women's voices as if they had died even in memory
And it's raining you as well marvelous encounters of my life
　O little drops
Those rearing clouds begin to neigh a whole universe of
　auricular cities
Listen if it rains while regret and disdain weep to an ancient
　music
Listen to the bonds fall off which hold you above and below
　　　　　　—Guillaume Apollinaire, "Il Pleut"
　　　　　　(translated by Roger Shattuck)

I was waiting for you. Please come back under the umbrella as if we were lovers.　—Yasunari Kawabata, *Palm-of-the-Hand Stories* (translated by Lane Dunlop)

Contents

ECSTATIC
CAHOOTS

Misterioso

"You're going to leave your watch on?"
"You're leaving on your cross?"

The Start of Something

Subway grates, steaming tamale carts, charcoal braziers roasting chestnuts, the breaths of the pedestrians outpacing stalled traffic, the chimneys Gil can't see from the window of the airline bus—all plume in the frigid air. It's cold enough for Gil to wear, for the first and only time, the salt-and-pepper woolen trousers he bought at an estate sale last summer. He'd stopped on a whim when he saw the sale sign, an excuse to tour a mansion that looked as if it once could have belonged to *The Great Gatsby*'s Tom Buchanan before he'd moved from Chicago's North Shore to Long Island "in a fashion," Fitzgerald wrote, "that rather took your breath away . . . he'd brought down a string of polo ponies from Lake Forest." Perhaps the deceased had left only debts, for the heirs, haughty with grief, were selling off the furnishings. Those there to buy spoke in subdued voices as if to seem less like scavengers. Gil browsed the sunlit rooms with no intention of buying anything, then in an upstairs bedroom he found an open cedar wardrobe filled with old, handsomely made men's clothes. He selected the trousers and held them up before a walnut-framed full-length mirror, and told himself he might wear them for cross-country skiing even though he hadn't skied in years. Later, when he tried them on at home, they fit as though they'd been made for him, causing Gil to wonder who the man who'd worn them had been. In one of the pockets there was an Italian coin dated

1921, and Gil thought it might be worth something to a collector. He kept it in a cuff-link box with spare buttons, a St. Christopher medal, a class ring, and cuff links he never wore. Even after he'd had the trousers dry-cleaned they smelled faintly of cedar.

The airline bus has nearly reached downtown when the woman in the seat across the aisle leans toward Gil and asks, "Are those lined?"

"Pardon?" he says.

"Are those lined? They're beautiful but they look itchy." Wings of dark glossy hair and a darker fur collar frame her narrow face. Her smile appears too broad for her, but attractive all the same.

"Partially," he says.

"Knee-length?"

"Not quite. Actually, they are a little itchy, but they're warm."

"They look right out of the Jazz Age. They've got that drape. I love anything from the twenties—music, furniture, the writers."

"Some of my favorite writers, all right," Gil says.

"They still read so alive! Like that newly liberated, modern world was just yesterday."

It sounds like she's speaking in quotes and Gil smiles as if to agree. Her hairstyle and the coat she's bundled in both suggest another time. The coat has a certain Goodwill-rack look that exempts a woman from the stigma of wearing fur. Gil has no idea what kind of fur it is. It matches the luster of her hair. He has the vague feeling they've met before, which makes talking to her effortless, but Gil doesn't say so for fear it would sound like a line. She'd know a man would remember meeting someone who looked like her.

"Where'd you find them?" she asks.

"At a kind of glorified garage sale."

"I didn't think they were new. When designers try to bring back a style they never quite get it right."

"They're the real deal all right, complete with little buttons for suspenders. I probably should be wearing suspenders."

"Not even half lined, though, huh? Bet it feels good to get them off." She smiles again as if surprised by what she has just said.

"You sure have an eye for clothes," Gil says.

"Don't I, though?"

Outside, snow settles on Chicago like a veil, as if it is the same veil of snow that was floating to earth earlier in the day when he boarded the plane in Minneapolis, returning from his father's funeral. The airline bus has stalled again in traffic. She's turned away, staring out the window. He doesn't know her name, has yet to ask where she's traveling from, if she lives in the city or is only visiting, let alone the facts of her personal life, but all the questions are already in motion between them.

Why not end here, without answers?

Aren't there chance meetings in every life that don't play out, stories that seem meant to remain ghostly, as faint and fleeting as the reflection of a face on the window of a bus? Beyond her face, snow swirls through steam from exhausts and manholes. Why not for this one time let beginning suffice, rather than insist on what's to come: the trip they'll take, before they know enough about each other, to Italy; those scenes in her apartment when she'll model her finds from vintage stores, fashions from the past he'll strip from her present body? Her name is Bea. She'll say they were fated to meet. They'll play at being reincarnated lovers from the First World War. Sometimes he's a soldier who died in the trenches, sometimes a young trumpet player poisoned by bathtub gin. Scene added to scene, fabrication to fabrication, until a year has passed and for a last time he visits her apartment in the Art Deco building on Dearborn with its curved, glowing glass brick windows. There's an out-of-place store on the ground floor that sells trophies—an inordinate number of them for bowling. Its burglar alarm, prone to going off after hours, as if the defeated have come by night to steal the prizes they can never win, is clanging again. She's been doing coke and tells him that in a dream she realized she's been left with two choices, one of which is to kill him. She laughs too gaily when she says it and he doesn't ask what the other choice is. She's mentioned that she's been "in touch" with her ex-boyfriend—a man who over nine years, with time-outs for affairs, has come and gone at will in her life, a relationship it took her a while to reveal fully because, she explained, she didn't want to give the impression she has a taste for "damaged men." If she's implying it's a relationship that redefines her, she has a point.

"Does he know about me?" Gil asked.

"I'd *never* tell him you exist," she said, her eyes suddenly anxious and her voice dropping to a whisper as if an omnipotent master might overhear.

"In touch" means Gil has noticed bruises when he hikes her skirt to kiss the curve of her bottom. She'll have asked for them, he knows, she'll have begged, "Leave your mark." The boyfriend is an importer, she says. He's a connected guy whose family owns a chain of pizza parlors. He carries a gun, which she says makes her feel safe, though what she really means is that she finds it thrilling, and when she disappears into her bedroom Gil isn't sure whether she'll emerge armed or wearing a chemise from the thirties that she's found at some flea market. No matter how often he strips the past from her body, she finds a way to wear it again. His impulse is to let himself out, but he doesn't want her—and for that matter, doesn't want himself—to be left with a final image of him running for his life. An escape might make it seem as if the choice in her dream were justified. He doesn't want to admit she's made him afraid, and so he sits and waits for her to reappear.

The heirs were selling off the furnishings. Gil browsed the sunlit rooms with no intention of buying anything, but in an upstairs bedroom he found an open wardrobe smelling of cedar. He held the trousers up before a full-length mirror that like everything else in the house wore a price, everything except the clothes—for those he'd have to bargain. His reflection, gazing back, fogged behind layers of dust, appeared ghostly. The trousers looked as if with a little tailoring they'd fit, and maybe he could wear them for cross-country skiing. How could he have known then that he was only at the start of something?

Drive

Lost: the hot-pink bullet from the spent cartridge of lip gloss he's found lodged between gearbox and seat. And the beat she always caught, chasing from station to station as they raced between red lights. The scent of summer evaporating at noon— coconut, sweat, the salt lick of her skin scorched against turquoise vinyl. Evening's perfume of broken heat, a tide of lawn sprinklers whipping through the dark as moons emerge: each neighborhood, each roof, each windowpane sending up its own. In the smaze of foundry chimneys, a tarnished spoon bent by telekinesis into a wedding band. Over a steeple, a halo missing a saint. Above the shimmering sweet-water sea, a tragic mask with a comic reflection. Or is it vice versa? There's one un-self-conscious about its pitted face; one with its own star in Hollywood; and another aloof, back turned as if boycotting tomorrow, the way that Miles Davis, circa *Kind of Blue*, would turn his back on the audience when he'd solo. And in the rearview mirror where it's always October, leaves blowing off like pages from an unfinished memoir . . .

"So, where to?" he'd ask.

"Baby, just drive."

I Never Told This to Anyone

I never told this to anyone—there wasn't anyone to tell it to—but when I was living with my uncle Kirby on the Edge—the edge of what I never knew for sure ("Just livin' on the Edge, don't worry *where*," Uncle Kirby would say)—a little bride and groom would come to visit me at night. Naturally, I never mentioned this to Uncle Kirby. He'd have acted as if I'd been playing with dolls. "A boy should play like the wild animals do—to practice survival," Uncle Kirby always said. "You wanna play, play with your Uzi."

The bride wore a white gown and silver slippers, and held a bouquet. The groom wore a top hat, tails, and spats. Their shoes were covered with frosting as if they'd walked through snow even though it was summer, June, when they first appeared. I heard a little pop—actually, more of a *pip!*—and there on my windowsill was the groom, pouring from a tiny champagne bottle. "Hi! I'm Jay and this is Trish," he said by way of introduction, adding confidentially, "We don't think of one another as Mr. and Mrs. yet."

They had tiny voices, but I could hear them clearly. "That's because we enunciate," Trish said. She was pretty.

"It's these formal clothes, Old Boy," Jay explained. "Put them on and you start to speak the King's English."

I remember the first night they appeared, and the nights

that followed, as celebrations—like New Year's Eve in June. There'd be big-band music on my shortwave—a station I could never locate except when Jay and Trish were over—and the *pip! pip! pip!* of miniature champagne bottles. You should have seen them dancing to "Out of Nowhere" in the spotlight my flashlight threw as it followed them across the floor. I'd applaud and Jay would kiss the bride. But each celebration seemed as if it would be the last.

"Off for the honeymoon, Old Boy," Jay would say with a wink as they left. He'd sweep Trish off her feet and carry her across the windowsill, and Trish would laugh and wave back at me, "*Ciao*—we'll be staying at the Motel d'Amore," and then she'd toss her small bouquet.

I didn't want them to go. Having their visits to look forward to made living on the Edge seem less desolate. Uncle Kirby noticed the change in me. "What's with *You*, lately?" he asked—*You* was sort of his nickname for me. "I mean, why *You* goin' round with rice in your pockets and wearin' that jazzbow tie? And what's with the old shoes and tin cans tied to the back fender a your bike? How *You* expect to survive that way when the next attack comes out a nowhere?"

I told him that dragging shoes and cans built up my endurance and the rice was emergency rations, and he left me alone, but I knew he was keeping an eye on me.

Luckily, no matter how often Jay and Trish said they were off, they'd show up again a few nights later, back on the windowsill, scraping the frosting from their shoes. And after a while, when they'd leave, walking away hand in hand into the shadows, Jay hooking his tux jacket over his shoulder rather than sweeping Trish off her feet, and Trish no longer carrying a bouquet to toss, neither of them would mention the honeymoon.

I didn't notice at first, but gradually the nights quieted

down. "A little more sedate an evening for a change," Jay would say. Trish, especially, seemed quieter. She said that champagne had begun making her dizzy. After dancing, she'd need a nap.

"*I get no kick from champagne*," Jay would tell her, raising his glass in a toast, "*but I get a kick out of you.*"

Trish would smile back, blow him a kiss, and then close her eyes. While she rested, Jay would sit and talk to me. He had a confidential way of speaking that made it seem as if he were always on the verge of revealing a secret, as if we shared the closeness of conspirators.

"Actually," he'd say, lowering his voice, "I still *do* get a kick from champagne, although it's nothing compared to what I feel around Trish. I never told this to anyone, but I married her simply because she brought magic into my life. The most beautiful songs on the radio came after she turned it on. She made the ordinary seem out of this world."

It wasn't until the sweltering nights of late summer, when Jay and Trish began to bicker and argue, that I realized how much things had changed. The two of them even looked different, larger somehow, as if they were outgrowing their now stained, shabby formal wear.

"I'm so tired of this ratty dress," Trish complained one evening.

"Now it's nag nag nag instead of *pip pip pip*," Jay replied. "And please don't say 'ratty.' You know how I despise the term."

Jay would harangue us on the subject of rodents in a way that reminded me of Uncle Kirby on the subject of Commies or certain ethnic groups. Jay had developed a bit of a potbelly and looked almost as if he were copying Trish, who was, by now, obviously expecting. *Expecting* was Trish's word. "Out of all the names they give it, don't you think 'expecting' sounds the prettiest?" she'd asked me once, surprising me, and I quickly agreed.

Their visits had become regular, and they showed up, increasingly ravenous, to dine on the morsels I'd filched from the supper table at Jay's suggestion. "Old Boy," Jay had said jokingly, "you can't just take the attitude of 'Let them eat cake.' After all, cake isn't a limitless resource, you know." I was glad to pilfer the food for them. It made mealtime an adventure. Stealing rations in front of Uncle Kirby wasn't easy.

After I served their little dinner, they'd stay and visit. Jay would sit drinking the beer that he'd devised a way of siphoning from Uncle Kirby's home brew.

"We could use a goddamn TV around this godforsaken boring place. It would be nice to watch a little bowling once in a while," Jay would gripe after he'd had a few too many.

"Maybe if you'd do something besides sitting around in your dirty underwear, drinking and belching, things wouldn't be so BORrrr-ing," Trish answered.

Once, after an argument that made Trish storm off in tears, Jay held his head and muttered, as if more to himself than to me, "I never told this to anyone, but me and the Mrs. *had* to get married."

By the time the leaves were falling, they had shed their wedding clothes. Trish wore a dress cut from one of my sweat socks, boots of bumblebee fur, and a hat made from a hummingbird's nest. Jay, bearded, a blue-jay feather poking from his top hat, dressed in the gray skin of an animal he refused to identify. He carried a knitting-needle spear, a bow he'd fashioned from the wishbone of a turkey, and a quiver of arrows— disposable hypodermic needles he'd scavenged from Uncle Kirby's supplies. He tipped each arrow in cottonmouth venom.

They never appeared now without first scavenging Uncle Kirby's storehoused supplies—at least, they called it scavenging. Uncle Kirby called it guerrilla warfare. He kept scrupulous inventories of his stockpiles, and detected, almost immediately, even the slightest invasion. Yet no matter how carefully he protected his supplies, Jay found ways to infiltrate his defenses.

Jay avoided poisons, raided traps, short-circuited alarms, picked locks, solved combinations, and carried off increasing amounts of Uncle Kirby's stuff. Even more than the loss of supplies, Jay's boldness and cleverness began to obsess Uncle Kirby.

"Hey, *You*," Uncle Kirby told me. "You're about to witness something you'll remember the rest a your life—short as that might be, given the way you're goin' at it. Kirby Versus the Varmints!"

It was the season to worry about supplies, to calculate the caches of food and jerry cans of water, the drums of fuel oil surrounded by barbed wire, the cords of scrap wood. Each night the wind honed its edge sharper in the bare branches. Each night came earlier. Lit by the flicker of my kerosene stove, Jay plucked the turkey bow as if it were an ancient single-stringed instrument. He played in accompaniment to the wind and to Trish's plaintive singing—an old folk song, she said, called "Expectations." The wind and the wandering melody reminded me of the sound of the ghostly frequencies on my shortwave. The ghostly frequencies were all I could pick up anymore, except for a station from far north on the dial that sounded as if it were broadcasting crows.

"Listen," Jay said, amused, "they're giving the crow financial report: 'Tuck away a little nest egg.'"

While we huddled around the stove, listening to the newscast of crows, Uncle Kirby was in his workshop, working late over an endless series of traps, baited cages, zappers. He invented the KBM (Kirby Better Mousetrap), the KRS (Kirby Rodent Surprise), and the KSPG (Kirby Small Pest Guillotine), which worked well enough in testing to cost him the tip of his little finger. Some of these inventions actually worked on rodents, and Uncle Kirby took to displaying his trophies by their tails. He devised trip wires, heat sensors, and surveillance monitors, but when Jay's raids continued despite Uncle Kirby's best efforts, the exhilaration of combat turned nasty. We were sitting at the supper table one evening over Kirby Deluxe—leftover meat loaf dipped in batter and deep-fried—and I'd stashed away a couple of bites along with a few canned peas for Jay and Trish when Uncle Kirby suddenly said, "All right, *You*, what's with the food in your cuffs?"

I tried to think of some reason he might believe, and realized we were beyond that, so I just hung my head over my plate.

"Look, *You*," Uncle Kirby said, shaking his bandaged hand in my face, "there's something mysterious going on here. I don't know what little game you're playin', but I think a preemptive strike's in order."

He left me trussed to a kitchen chair, and that night he handcuffed my ankle to the bunk. It was the night of the first snow. Jay appeared late, kicking the snow from his moleskin boots.

"Trish asked me to say goodbye for her, Old Boy," Jay said. "It's getting a bit barbarous around here, you know."

I turned my face to the wall.

"She said to tell you that she wants to name the baby after you, unless it's a girl, of course, in which case Old Boy wouldn't be appropriate."

I didn't laugh. When you're trying to hold back tears, laughing can suddenly make you cry.

"This isn't like us going off on a honeymoon, Old Boy," Jay said. He was busy picking the lock on the handcuffs with his knitting-needle spear. "We never did get to the Motel d'Amore, but that time we spent here in summer, that *was* the honeymoon. I never told this to anyone, but maybe someday you'll understand, if you're lucky enough to meet someone who'll make you feel as if your heart is wearing a tuxedo, as if your soul is standing in a chapel in the moonlight and your life is rushing like a limo running red lights, you'll understand how one day you open your eyes and it's as if you find yourself standing on top of a wedding cake in the middle of the road, an empty highway, without a clue as to how you got there, but then, that's all part of coming out of nowhere, isn't it?"

When they didn't return the next night, I knew I'd never see them again, and I picked the lock as I'd seen Jay do with the knitting needle he'd left behind, and cut the cans and shoes off my bike and took off, too. It wasn't easy. Uncle Kirby had booby-trapped the perimeter. I knew he'd come looking for me, that, for him, finding me would seem like something out of the only story he'd ever read me—"The Most Dangerous Game." But I knew about my own secret highway—I never told this to anyone—a crumbling strip of asphalt, a shadow of an old two-lane, overgrown, no more of it left than a peeling center stripe through a swamp. I rode that center stripe as if balanced on the edge of a blade. It took me all the way to here.

Fridge

At midnight the expedition of the bride and groom arrives at the Fridge and pauses to get its bearings from the pale, arctic twenty-watt sun before proceeding across a border there is no need to map.

Before them lies the taiga where the wolf vowel of wind penetrates the heart with the aim of a winter draft through an uncaulked bedroom window—a draft that feels its way down corridors of sleep, its Freon breath scented with the rotten moss of unmade salads and wilted scallions.

And beyond the taiga, a tundra stretches that, from its smell, must be the snow-blinding white of sour milk.

There's a sadness locked away here that emerges slowly like the freezer-burned flavors from some glacial past molded into cubes of ice. There's a cheese never meant to be blue. There are undesired dreams and memories preserved in an isolation in which dream and memory have become indistinguishable from one another, both smoldering like ghosts of cold around a temperature dial forced beyond its lowest subtraction.

Here are the silent regions of rock-hard meat frozen into obscene postures like the dead around Stalingrad, regions where body heat has vanished beneath a crust of frost, where breath hangs although the breathers are long gone; dangerous regions where, even after the plug has been pulled, love can still be smothered as if it were a child playing hide-and-seek in a junked appliance.

Midwife

It was Martin who kidnapped the French doll with her bald skull fractured beneath a wig of spun gold and her chipped blue eyes that clattered up into her brain. He kidnapped her from his cousin, Terra, after Terra had raised the doll's red velvet frock and pulled down its yellowed muslin undies in order to demonstrate the differences in anatomy between them. She had asked Martin, who was younger than she was, if he wanted to see what girls looked like and when he said okay Terra led him into her bedroom and closed the door behind them.

"It's too bright," she said. "Pull down the shades."

Martin pulled down the shades, and now the room smelled of the shades as well as the dozens of bottles of perfume atop Terra's dresser.

"It could be a sin. I thought you wanted to be an altar boy someday and wear a lace surplice. Are you sure you want to see?" Terra asked in a whisper.

"I do," Martin whispered back.

Terra threw herself down on her bed and lay seized by a fit of laughter. When she recovered, she brought the French doll down from its place on a bookshelf.

It wasn't her favorite doll, Terra said. It was too old-fashioned and there was no wardrobe for it, so it wore the same dingy clothes day after day. The doll's name was Terri.

Terri from Paris. It rhymed if you pronounced *Paris* like the French. Terri from Paris was special because she'd been the favorite doll of Terra's mother when she was a girl. And before that Terri had been the favorite of Terra's grandmother. Terra had never met her grandmother.

Terri from Paris ran in the family, Terra said. Terra's father had told her that someday Terra would pass the doll down to her own daughter.

"That's why you took her from Mom, isn't it?" her father had asked. "Because you wanted to pass her on to your own little girl."

"Mom forgot she gave her to me," Terra had answered.

Actually, her mother had never given her Terri. While her mother was alive the doll had lived in a hatbox on top of a shelf in her mother's closet. Terra told Martin that she'd lied to her father, because she wasn't about to agree to passing a doll on to a little girl of her own since she had no intention of having a little girl of her own.

Terra had never met her grandmother because, like Terra's mother, her grandmother had died young, of breast cancer. When Terra's mother was dying, she'd asked that the doll be buried with her. Terra sneaked Terri from Paris out of the coffin.

"So you want to see something I discovered?" Terra asked Martin.

This time Martin said nothing. He didn't want to be laughed at again.

Terra showed him anyway. She lifted the doll's frock and pulled down the yellowed muslin underpants.

"I don't know if my mother ever took these underpants down, but maybe it's why she kept Terri in a hatbox," Terra said. The space between the doll's legs had been cracked as if someone had tapped it with a hammer. In the middle of the crack a jagged hole opened on the hollow interior of the doll.

The hole was surrounded with the same cotton candy frizz of gold hair as once seemed to grow from the doll's head before it became unglued and now looked like a wig.

"I think my uncle Bella did that," Terra said. "I think he did that when he was a boy. He always tickles me. I hate him."

Martin kept the potato even more secret than he did the doll. Wearing the doll's golden wig, the potato was hidden away behind the tubes in his makeshift dollhouse, an ancient TV set half gutted in the basement. The potato troubled Martin, but Martin couldn't forget it or leave it alone. At night, while the family slept, he crept down into the basement, turned on the bare bulb above the workbench, and clamped the potato in the vise. Sometimes he put his own finger in the vise and tightened it to see how long he could take the pain. He selected screws and nails of various sizes from the mayonnaise jars in which his father had them organized. Then he screwed and hammered them into the potato. He daubed the wounds they made with Mercurochrome from the tiny clotted bottle that had been stored away on the top shelf of the medicine chest for as long as he could remember. Some of the Mercurochrome ran in streaks down the wrinkled potato skin and dripped like orange drops of blood to the dusty floor.

Finally, he stripped off its wig and buried the potato in a narrow corridor of sunless dirt between the house and the garage. He could bury it, but he couldn't stop worrying about it. So he found himself digging it up just at dusk one Sunday after dinner. The screws were already rusting, the nails turning black, festering. Sickly white fingers sprouted from the eyes. He squirted it with lighter fluid and watched it char in a ball of blue flames, then he peed out the fire.

After that it was no good simply burying it again. He put it in a brown bag that he taped shut with tape from the roll of white adhesive tape that had been stored on the top shelf of the medicine chest for as long as he could remember. Whenever he swung the mirrored door of the medicine chest shut he would watch for his face to appear, trying to catch its expression before his reflection met his eyes. When the mirror swung he could feel his eyes roll like a doll's, minus the clatter, but he couldn't catch that eye roll happening to his reflection.

It was Sunday night. Martin stood before the mirror on the medicine chest. He'd taken his clothes off and was daubing himself with Mercurochrome around his wounds—his nipples, his navel, the tip of his wiener. With the tiny scissors his father used to clip hairs from his nostrils, Martin snipped strips off the roll of adhesive tape and taped them over his Mercurochromed scars. Orange streaks ran from the tape. It reminded him of Christ on the cross and he stretched his arms out pretending the nails were in his palms. Then he taped his mouth. He wanted to imagine what the doll would feel in the time to come when, staked to the workbench, she would give birth to the potato.

Confession

Father Boguslaw was the priest I always waited for, the one whose breath through the thin partition of the confessional reminded me of the ventilator behind Vic's Tap. He huffed and smacked as if in response to my dull litany of sins, and I pictured him slouched in his cubicle, draped in vestments, the way he sat slumped in the back entrance to the sacristy on cold mornings before saying morning mass—hungover, sucking an unlit Pall Mall, exhaling smoke.

Once, his head thudded against the wooden box.

"Father," I whispered, "Father," but he was out, snoring. I knelt wondering what to do, until he finally groaned and hacked himself awake.

As usual, I'd saved the deadly sins for last: the lies and copied homework, snitching drinks, ditching school, hitchhiking, which I'd been convinced was an offense against the Fifth Commandment, which prohibited suicide. Before I reached the dirty snapshots of Korean girls, stolen from the dresser of my war-hero uncle, Uncle Al, and still unrepentantly cached behind the oil shed, Father B knocked and said I was forgiven.

As for Penance: "Go in peace, my son, I'm suffering enough today for both of us."

The Kiss

She lies bluish in a puddle that looks like it has seeped through her skin. The Lifeguard with bleached hair and white zinc cream nearly washed off his nose, wearing a soaked red tank top with a white cross on the front and his name—well, his nickname—*Mars*, on the back, is giving her the kiss of life. He holds her nose pinched, comes up for air himself, and then fits his mouth over hers. It sounds as if he's blowing up a rubber raft.

She just kept swimming when he blew his whistle. He rose in his tower chair and blew repeated blasts as he watched her stroking out past the buoys. By the time he'd raced across the sand to his boat, scattering shorebirds as he went, and was rowing out after her with the gulls screaming and swirling overhead as if he was chumming, she was going under.

A sunburned guy in cutoffs, a backward baseball cap, and mirror-lensed sunglasses pushes through the crowd repeating, "I'm a doctor, excuse me, I'm a doctor." The doctor kneels beside her, feeling for a pulse, and the Lifeguard, between breaths, asks him, "Who the fuck are you really?"

"A med student, just keep doing what you're doing."

The Lifeguard leans back toward her lips but at that moment a cough jolts her body, she spits up water and snot, and opens her eyes.

Now that she is no longer a corpse, the boys in the crowd

press in to memorize the shriveled nipple of the breast popped over her hot-pink bikini. An ambulance, its siren dropped to a pitch that resonates more in molars than ears, churns toward them across the sand.

"Why'd you do it?" the Lifeguard asks softly.

The med student scowls at him, shakes his head in disapproval, then removes his sunglasses as if it is important to his bedside manner that the girl sees his eyes, and asks, "Feel dizzy? Nauseous? Do you want to throw up?"

"You're so pretty . . . so young . . . why?" the Lifeguard repeats, nudging the med student aside, although, even as he asks, he knows the question is wrong. But the invisible imprint of the kiss on his lips is shaping his words. There's a sudden, compelling bond between him and this girl just back from the dead, an intimacy of a kind he's never felt before, an urgency to keep saving her that is ruining his judgment. He has to resist the desire to take her in his arms, hold her close, and resume kissing her. For the moment whispering is as close as he can get.

"Why'd you do it?" he whispers, as if to reassure her that her secret will be safe with him.

"Do what?" the girl asks, and looks at him dazed, lost, her trembling fingers tugging at her tangled, waterlogged hair.

It's clear from her confused blue eyes that she's brought back nothing she can share, no forbidden secrets to confide to the living. She doesn't remember where she's just been; her few moments of death are harder for her to recall than a fleeting dream. She doesn't remember the mouth on hers that brought her back, or his breath searching for her through the darkened corridors of her body, trying dead end after dead end until he found a pathway to her will. She doesn't remember the kiss. It has remained a part of her total absence from herself. Soon, no one will remember it but the Lifeguard, and he's right to suspect that it's the one kiss he'll recall for the rest of his life.

The connection between them is slipping away and the Lifeguard lets it go as if releasing her body back to the water.

"Any of you her friends?" he asks, looking into the crowd that's reflected on the med student's sunglasses.

She accepts a half-smoked cigarette from a hand in the crowd, and the Lifeguard, still able to feel the terrible press of coldness against his lips, rises from his knees in the sand. He stands watching, no longer necessary, as they bundle her in a faded beach towel, and she leaves without so much as a thank-you, or a wave goodbye.

Córdoba

While we were kissing, the leather-bound *Obras completas* opened to a photo of Federico García Lorca with a mole prominent beside a sideburn of his slicked-back hair, slid from her lap to the jade silk couch, and hit the Chinese carpet with a muffled thud.

While we were kissing, the winter wind known locally as the Hawk soared off the lake on vast wings of snow.

While we were kissing, verbs went uncommitted to memory.

Her tongue rolled *r*'s against mine, but couldn't save me from failing Spanish. We were kissing, but her beloved Federico, to whom she'd introduced me on the night we'd first met, was not forgotten. *Verde que te quiero verde. Green I want you green. Verde viento, verdes ramas. Green wind, green branches.* Hissing radiator heat. Our breaths elemental, beyond translation like the shrill of the Hawk outside her sweated, third-story windows. *Córdoba. Lejana y sola,* she translated between kisses, *Córdoba. Far away and alone.* With our heads full of poetry, the drunken, murderous Guardias Civiles were all but knocking at the door.

> *Aunque sepa los caminos*
> *yo nunca llegaré a Córdoba.*

Though I know the roads
I will never reach Córdoba.

Shaking off cold, her stepfather, Ray Ramirez, came home from his late shift as manager of the Hotel Lincoln. He didn't disturb us other than to announce from the front hall: "Hana, tell David, it's a blizzard out there! He better go while there's still buses!"

"It's a blizzard out there," Hana told me.

It was then we noticed the white roses in a green vase that her mother, who resembled Lana Turner, and who didn't much like me, must have set there while we were kissing. We hadn't been aware of her bringing them in. Hana and I looked at each other: she was still flushed, our clothes were disheveled. We hadn't merely been kissing. She shrugged and buttoned her blouse. *Verte desnuda es comprender el ansia de la lluvia. To see you naked is to comprehend the desire of rain.* I picked her volume of Lorca from the floor and set it beside the vase of flowers, and slipped back into the loafers I'd removed to curl up on the jade couch.

"I better go."

"It's really snowing. God! Listen to that wind! Do you have a hat? Gloves? All you have is that jacket."

"I'll be fine."

"Please, at least take this scarf. For me. So I won't worry."

"It smells like you."

"It smells like Anias."

At the door we kissed goodbye as if I were leaving on a journey.

"Are you sure you're going to be all right?"

Hana followed me into the hallway. We stopped on each stair down to the second-floor landing to kiss goodbye. She snuggled into my leather jacket. The light on the second-floor landing was out.

"Good luck on your Spanish test. Phone me, so I know you got home safe, I'll be awake thinking of you," she called down to me.

"*Though I know the roads I will never reach Córdoba.*"

"Just so you reach Rogers Park."

I stepped from her doorway onto Buena. It pleased me— amazed me, actually—that Hana should live on the only street in Chicago, at least the only street I knew of, with a Spanish name. Her apartment building was three doors from Marine Drive. That fall, when we first began seeing each other, I would take the time to walk up Marine Drive on my way home. I'd discovered a viaduct tunnel unmarked by graffiti that led to a flagstone grotto surrounding a concrete drinking fountain with four spouts. Its icy water tasted faintly metallic, of rust or moonlight, and at night the burble of the fountain transformed the place into a Zen garden. Beyond the grotto and a park, the headlights on Lake Shore Drive festooned the autumn trees. For a moment, I thought of going to hear the fountain purling under the snow, but the Hawk raked my face and the frosted trees quavered. *Green branches, green wind.* I raised the collar of my jacket and wrapped her green chenille scarf around my throat. Even in the numbing wind I could smell perfume.

By the time I slogged the four blocks to Broadway, it wasn't Lorca but a line by Emily Dickinson that expressed the night: *zero at the bone.* No matter which direction I turned, the swirling wind was in my face. My loafers felt packed with snow. Broadway was deserted. I cowered in the dark doorway of a dry cleaner's, peeking out now and again and stamping my feet. The snow-plastered bus stop sign hummed in the gusts, but there wasn't a bus visible in either direction. A cab went by and, though I wasn't sure I could make the fare, I tried to flag it down. It didn't stop. The snow had drifted deep enough so that the cabbie wouldn't risk losing momentum. Finally, to warm up, I crossed the street to a corner bar called the Buena Chimes. Its blue neon sign looked so faint I doubted the place was open. If it was, I expected it to be empty, which I hoped would allow the bartender to take pity on me. I was twenty, a year shy of legal drinking age.

The cramped, low-lit space was packed, or so it first appeared. Though only three men sat at the bar, they were so massive they seemed to fill the room. Their conversation stopped when I came in. I'd heard the rumor that players for the Chicago Bears sometimes drank there but hadn't believed it, probably because I'd heard it from Hana's stepfather, Ray, who'd also told me that as a cliff diver in Acapulco he once collided with a tiger shark, whose body now hung in the lobby of the Grand Mayan Hotel. With all of Rush Street waiting to toast them, why would Bears drink at a dump like the Buena Chimes?

I undid the green scarf that I'd tied around my head babushka-style, and edged onto a stool by the door—as respectful a distance as possible from their disrupted conversation, but it wasn't far enough.

"Sorry, kid, private party," the bartender said.

"Any idea if the buses are running?" I asked.

"We're closed." He seemed morose. So did the Bears at the bar, who sat in silence as if what they had to say were too confidential to be uttered in the presence of a stranger. The team was having a losing season.

"Buy the kid a shot," one of the Bears said.

"Whatever you say, Jimbo," the bartender replied. He set a shot glass before me and, staring into my face rather than at the glass, filled it perfectly to the brim. Each man has his own way to show he's nobody's fool, and pouring shots without looking at the glass was the bartender's: he knew I was underage.

"Hit me, too, Sambo," Jimbo said, and when the bartender filled his glass, the tackle or linebacker or whatever Jimbo was raised the teeny shot glass in my direction. "This'll warm you up. Don't say I never bought you nothing," he said, and we threw back our whiskeys.

"Much thanks," I said.

"Now get your puny ass out of here," Jimbo told me.

Back outside, I hooded my head in the green scarf and watched a snowplow with whirling emergency lights scuff by and disappear up Broadway. Waiting was futile. I decided to walk to the L station on Wilson. Rather than wade the drifted sidewalks, I followed the ruts the snowplow left in the street. I trudged head down, not bothering to check for traffic until I heard a horn behind me. Headlights burrowed through the blizzard. The beams appeared to be shooting confetti. The car—a Lincoln, maybe—sported an enormous, toothy grille. Whatever its make, the style was what in my old neighborhood was called a pimpmobile. I stepped from the ruts to give it room to pass. It slowed to a stop. A steamed window slid down.

"Need a ride, hombre?"

I got in, my lips too frozen for more than a "thanks." The rear wheels spun. I sat shivering, afraid I'd have to leave the blast of the heater in order to push that big-ass boat out of the snow.

"You can do it, baby," the driver said as if urging a burro. I was tempted to caution that giving it gas would only dig us in deeper, but knew to keep such opinions to myself. "Come on, baby!" He ripped the floor shift into reverse, slammed it back into drive, back into reverse, and into drive again. "Go, go, you got it," and as if it were listening, the car rocked forward, grabbed, and kept rolling.

"Thought for a second we were stuck," I said.

"No way, my friend, and hey, you're here to push, but not to worry, there's no stopping Lino tonight."

I unwound the scarf from my head and massaged my frozen nose and ears.

"Yo, man, you wearing perfume?" he asked.

"It's the scarf," I said.

"You in that scarf, man! When I saw you in the street, I thought some poor broad was out alone, you know? I told myself, Lino, the world is full of babes tonight. Where you headed, my friend?"

"Rogers Park," I said. "Just off Sheridan." I couldn't stop shivering.

"Man, you'd a had a tough time getting there. Whole city's shut down. What you doing out so late? Getting a little, dare I ask?" He smiled conspiratorially. His upturned mustache attached to his prominent nose moved independently of his smile.

"Drinking. With the Bears," I added.

"You mean like the football Bears?"

"Yeah, Jimbo and the guys."

"Over at the Buena Chimes, man?"

"How'd you know?"

"Everybody knows they drink there. You got the shakes, man? Lino got the cure—pop the glove compartment."

I pressed the button and the glove compartment flopped open. An initialed silver flask rested on a ratty-looking street map. Beneath the map I could see the waffled gray handle of a small-caliber gun. I closed the glove compartment, and we passed the flask between us in silence.

"What are we drinking?" I asked. It had an oily licorice taste with the kick of grain alcohol—not what I expected.

"We're drinking to a night that's going to be a goddamn legend, hombre. The kind of night that changes your life." He took a swig for emphasis, then passed the flask to me. "To our lucky night—hey, I'm spreading the luck around, right?—your luck I picked you up, mine cause I got picked up."

"Huh?" I wasn't sure I liked the sound of that, and held off on taking my swig.

"Check this out." He fished into his shirt pocket, handed me a folded scrap of paper, and flicked on the overhead interior light.

The paper unfolded into a lipsticked impression of a kiss, a phone number inscribed in what looked like eyebrow pencil, and the words, *Call me tonight. Tonight* underlined.

"You ever seen a woman so hot you didn't want to stare but couldn't take your eyes off her? I don't mean some bimbo at a singles bar. I'm in the Seasons and I see this almost-blonde in a tight green dress. She's drinking with this guy and don't look happy. He leans over and whispers something in her ear, and whatever he said, it's like, you know, an eye-roller. She turns away from him and as she's rolling her eyes to no one in particular she catches me staring. She got these beautiful eyes. And I roll my eyes, too, and just for a sec she smiles, then goes back to her drink. Doesn't look at me again, but five minutes later she gets up to go to the ladies', and when she does I see that green dress has a plunging back. Sexiest dress I ever seen. She walks right by my table, and on her way back she drops the note."

He reached for the flask, took a hit, and flicked out the interior light. Blowing snow reflected opaque in the headlights; it was hard to see ahead. He flicked the headlights off, too. "Better without them," he said. "Ain't no oncoming traffic to worry about."

We'd driven blocks, passed the L station on Wilson, and the little Asia Town on Argyle, ignored all the traffic signals on Broadway to keep our momentum, and hadn't seen another car.

We were approaching Sheridan Road. I was finally warmed up, though my feet were still numb. He took another swallow—he was drinking two to my one—and passed the flask. It was noticeably lighter.

"You believe in love at first sight, man? Romantic crap, right? An excuse some people need to get laid. I'm thirty-four years old and that's what I always thought, but now I don't know. Or it's more like I *do* know. I know what's going to happen like it already happened. This snowstorm, the whole city shut down, you know, like destiny, man, destiny in a green dress."

"*Verde que te quiero verde*," I said.

"Say what?"

"Lines from a poem."

"My mind keeps going over how she rolled her eyes and suddenly we're staring at each other and boom, across a crowded room." He rolled his droopy eyes to demonstrate. "What's that old song—my Pops used to sing it with an Italian accent: *Some-a enchanted-a evening you may see a stranger . . .*"

I'd wondered why he stopped to give me a ride—out of kindness or because he'd mistaken me for a woman alone, or to have someone along who could push, in case we got stuck. I recalled a Chekhov story from a Lit class called "Grief," about a horse-cab driver who on a freezing Moscow night tries to tell his story to every passenger he picks up, but rather than listen, each person tells him his own story instead. Finally, near dawn, as he unharnesses his pony, the cabdriver tells the story he's been trying all night to tell—that his little daughter has just died—to his pony. Lino was driving with a story to tell, not about grief or love or even male vanity. It was about luck, and he needed someone to hear it.

"What you going to do?" I asked him.

"What am I going to do? I'm going to call her! She's hot, man. She's waiting. She wants me. It's a sin if a woman wants you and you don't go. You ever had anything like this happen to you? What would you do?"

"Probably worry about what to say for openers."

"You could recite a poem. I got the perfect line, man. I'm going to ask her: What did that guy whisper to make you roll your eyes? See, that's what I meant about destiny. I already know what to say."

"You know her answer?"

"Man, that's the fun part. I know she'll answer, but not what. I know we'll kiss, but not how she kisses, I know she'll give me some tit right off, but not what kind of nipples she has—some guys are tit-men, I'm a nipple-man—or what perfume she wears, or what her name is. I know she's probably home by now waiting for the call, but I won't know till she picks up that phone what her voice sounds like. Just one little scrap of paper, and a lifetime history of questions. You can't really tell nothing from her handwriting. Let me see that."

"I gave it back to you," I said.

"No, man, you didn't give it back."

"Yes, I did. I handed it back when you turned the overhead light out, right before you flicked the headlights out. I handed it back to you blocks ago."

"You didn't, man, you never gave it to me."

"Check your pockets."

He checked his shirt pocket and the pockets of his topcoat. "I wouldn't have put it in my topcoat, man, you still got it. Empty your jacket pockets, *cabrón*."

I did as he asked. There wasn't anything but white petals from one of the roses Hana must have slipped in a pocket. She did things like that.

"What you trying to pull, my friend? This is how you repay me for saving your ass from the cold? If you think that babe is going to be a slut for any jerk who calls her up you're crazy. You ain't ready for a woman like that."

"I didn't take it, man."

He braked hard and the car swerved and came to a stop in the middle of the street. He flicked the overhead light on. "Get up, *cabrón*, maybe you're sitting on it." I rose in my seat and so did he. It wasn't on the seats. "Check the floor." We looked on the smeary floor mats and felt under the seats. "Check the bottom of your shoes."

"It's got to be here," I said.

"I'm going to ask you polite one more time, you going to give me that phone number?"

"I gave it to you. Why would I take it? I got my own girl. She insisted I wear her scarf."

"I thought you said you were drinking with the Bears. More bullshit, huh? Listen carefully, *cabrón*. Last fucking time—a simple yes or no."

His droopy brown eyes stared hard into my face. I said nothing. He unscrewed the flask and drained it. "Excuse me, man, I want to put this back." He reached past me, popped the glove compartment, and I was out of the car, running up Sheridan in the headlights he flicked on, bounding drifts, zigzagging along the sidewalk, hoping I'd be a harder target to hit. I could hear the tires whining behind me. He'd probably tried to give it gas and run me down and now the car was stuck. I could hear it grinding from a block away, and stopped to look back. He was trying to rock it from reverse back to drive, but just digging it in deeper. I actually thought of going back and saying, *Look, man, you were kind enough to give me a ride, would I have come back to push you out if I'd stolen your phone number?* It was a nice thought, but one that could get me killed. Instead, feeling light on my frozen feet despite the drifted sidewalks, I jogged four more blocks up Sheridan Road, checking at each corner to make sure he wasn't following me. The snow fell more slowly and the wind had let up some, but I could barely see his headlights five blocks back in the haze of snow when I turned onto my street.

In my studio apartment, I kicked off my loafers, stripped off my frozen socks, and, not bothering to remove my jacket, I sat in the dark on my one stuffed chair, clutching my soles in my palms and watching the snow gently float in the aura of the streetlight visible from my third-story window. The surge of lightness I'd felt running down Sheridan had left me shaky. *Zero at the bone.* Finally, I felt recovered enough to switch on the lamp and slip off my jacket. I'd promised to call Hana. She'd be asleep with the phone under the pillow beside her, so that its ring wouldn't wake anyone else. What time is it? she'd ask in a groggy voice, and I'd say getting on to one, and she'd say she worried about me getting home, and I'd tell her Córdoba was easy next to tonight. I'd thank her for the loan of her scarf. I'd have frozen without it.

It wasn't until I unwound it from around my neck that I noticed the scrap of paper caught in the chenille. I unfolded the note and there was the kiss and the phone number in eyebrow pencil.

I sat in the stuffed chair, my feet wedged under the cushion, dialed, and when the phone began to ring, I flicked the lamp off again and watched the snow. It rang several times, which didn't surprise me; I didn't expect anyone to answer. The surprise came as I was about to hang up, when someone lifted the receiver, but said nothing as if waiting for me to speak.

"I hope it's not too late to call?" I said.

"That all depends," a woman's voice answered.

"On what?"

"On who you are and what you have in mind. Coming over?"

"I can't tonight. The city's shut down. My car's stuck in a snowdrift."

"Then why did you bother to call?"

"I wanted to hear your voice. To see if you're real?"

"That's a strange thing to say. Are you real?"

"No," I said, "actually, I'm not."

"At least you know that," she said, "which puts you ahead of the game. Most unreal men—which is the vast majority—don't know they aren't, and those few that do usually can't bear to admit it. So there's still a chance that hopefully some night years to come, you'll have a different answer. Good luck with that." The phone clicked.

I listened to it buzz before hanging up. If I rang again, I knew she wouldn't answer. I sat with the soles of my feet in my hands, rubbing the warmth back into them, waiting to call Hana, thinking of all the years to come, still young enough to wonder who I'd be.

Ordinary Nudes

She stands before the full-length mirror that's framed by the bedroom door, observing how her nipples, navel, and the delta of copper hair, which has grown back at the confluence of her thighs, shimmer in the dusky light. Her reflection dimples and ripples like the surface of a pond where fish rise to feed on a mayfly hatch. Imagine his wonder when in the years to come he'll realize that she was not to be confused with ordinary nudes—not some nymph frolicking along the shore, or goddess ascending from sea foam, or ballerina poised to wade into her morning bath. Those photographs she let him take, kept in a drawer, beneath his underwear as if hidden in the depths, will age as she does.

Current

Beside a pool along the green bank of a river, a faun reaches through the transparent reflection of his nakedness and catches hold of the current.

Or the current has seized him, coiling his wrist like a submerged line. A rope of rough hemp slick with moss, the kind of rope that's left a groove across the shoulders of civilizations, a rope that might harness slaves to the giant stones of the pyramids or connect the collars of captives as they march to the auction block, a hangman's rope, a rope for tying rebels to the whipping post, for binding witches and heretics to fire, for fettering the mad as if they were barn animals, for dangling suicides at the crossroads, a rope with which the conquistadores might set their anchor like a fishhook in the maw of the New World, a rope whose knot even the great Houdini could not undo.

The faun, his muscles bulging, strains against the current, and a silently exploding cloud of scum rises as if he's engaged in landing a monstrous fish, some bottom-feeder with a beard of barbels and popping eyes, dislodged from its underwater cave yet refusing to be yanked up into dappled sunlight.

As the faun struggles, the bank beneath his feet bunches like a fabric pulled out of shape by a loose thread. Its pattern of cattails and reeds, ferns and water lilies is slowly drawn together until distinctions among species disappear in a tangle of green. He pulls as frogs hop and turtles crawl from their devastated kingdom, and even the hovering dragonflies no longer recognize where they were hatched. He continues to pull, and farther off, a field, despite the weight of cedars, moves like a Persian rug beneath a grand piano.

The silent tug-of-war beneath the sun's lidless eye exhausts him—but not in a way that makes him sweat and pant for breath. Instead he's filled with a sudden, drowsy lethargy, and collapses beside the small harp he has dropped in order to grasp the current. As he sinks deeper into sleep, first the field and then the riverbank gradually relax, reassuming their recognizable shapes. The turtles and frogs return to their stations, dragonflies ride the shimmering air. He has begun to dream.

His dream spreads across the pooling river where his reflection floated before he disturbed it. In his dream a young woman bathes amid water hyacinths, and the dream itself seems even more exposed and vulnerable than the reflection of his naked body. Damselflies dip to it and alight for a glistening instant. Naiads of mayflies and water skaters dimple its placid surface, while circles expand from where darting minnows have kissed its shadowy underside. A breeze scented with cedar blows through the harp strings, making music. Kingfishers, egrets, and blue herons wheel and land, pacing around his bare body with the marionette strides of waterbirds. Even the loon's manic laughter echoing eerily through the cypress swamp doesn't wake him. And the current that he still clutches now flows through his fist, unraveling between his fingers like a braid coming loose down the spine of a virgin.

A Confluence of Doors

After days of drifting, the man arrives at a confluence of doors. Had he been adrift on a river instead of the ocean, it would seem as if he were encountering a logjam from some long-removed past when the virgin forests were being dismantled. Had he been adrift on city streets, he might have come upon these doors hammered up into a makeshift barrier, a dead end walling off the wrecking site of a condemned neighborhood.

From afar, their surfaces shimmer like an ice floe. As he floats closer they appear like a Sargasso Sea of wood instead of weed, a gigantic deck without a ship, a floating graveyard where doors come to rest, undulating with the gentle roll of the sea.

The man rises unsteadily, shading his eyes, balancing his weight in the gently rocking life raft. From where he stands, the doors appear tightly butted against one another like pieces of a gigantic puzzle. He can see doors of all designs—plain and ornate, hardwood and pine, some varnished, others painted, all of them weathered. Some have peepholes, some have mail slots, some have numbers, foot plates, knockers, locks, doorknobs of brass, wrought iron, glass, and some have only puttied holes where the doorknobs are missing. He can't see any hinges. The doors are all floating with their outsides up, facing the sky, and their insides facedown in salt water.

He paddles the raft along what seems the shore of a strange, uncharted island, and moors it, carefully securing the line to the knocker of what must once have been the stately door of a mansion. He bellies from the raft and stands, accustoming his legs to bearing his weight again and to the slight roll. With each undulation of the sea a clear film of water washes across the surface of the doors, glossing them like a fresh coat of shellac. As he walks he can hear the slosh of his cuffs and the creak of his footsteps on the warped wood. It's too quiet. He'd hoped for the bustle of nesting seabirds, sunning turtles, fish leaping up and plopping back at the edge where the water laps. He'd hoped, at least, for the company of his shadow. After so many days at sea, he was looking forward to having a shadow again, a real shadow, with its long legs striding in time to his own. When he can't detect one, he is suddenly, inordinately disappointed. All that keeps him from weeping is his realization that, in isolation, his emotions have grown childish. He has begun each new day of drifting by promising himself that, whatever happens, he will not panic, and that promise now restores his composure.

He walks farther inland, a single figure on a wooden plain, and then whirls as if he's heard someone following him. For a moment he could swear that he's heard footfalls other than his own. Of course, there's no one there, just isolation playing its tricks. But, standing quietly, he hears a sound that can't be ascribed either to his own footfalls or to the rhythmic slap of water along the shoreline. He hears it again—a steady, nearly imperceptible knocking.

He proceeds inland and now not only can he hear the sound, but he can feel its vibrations through the soles of his bare feet. Each door he steps on knocks back from the other side. From the elegant doors there comes a polite rap, from the ornate, stately doors a firmer, more commanding knock, and from the nicked, peeling doors comes a battering of knuckles that threatens to build into an abusive pounding.

The farther he walks, the more insistent the knocking

becomes. It is no longer restricted to the doors he steps on. The doors all around him have picked up the sound—each door with its own particular rap, its own pitch and rhythm, its own demand or plea, though he can't tell if he is hearing the blows of someone desperately trying to enter, or of someone locked in and trying to escape.

The barrage of fists and feet against wood is becoming deafening. The flat landscape of doors trembles as if straining at hinges he can't see. He seizes the knob of a plain pine door and tries to yank it open, but it's locked. He tries a charred-looking black door on which the darkened paint has been buckled by intense heat, a door that sounds ready to split under a rain of blows, but it is locked as firmly as if it has been nailed shut.

"Hello!" he yells. "Who's there?"

There's no answer except for the knocking, which becomes still more furious.

All the doors are locked. He knows this without trying them one by one. They are shut tight, as if the weight of fathoms, the pressure of a deep ocean trench, is holding them closed. And even amid the pounding he has an odd flash of memory: how, as a child, he would tease his younger brother mercilessly, until his brother, who had a terrible temper, lost all control and came at him with a baseball bat or a hammer or a knife. He would run from his brother through the house into the basement, or slam himself behind a shed door, holding it shut while his brother pulled furiously from the other side, shouting, "I'll kill you!" When he couldn't force it open, his brother would expend his anger by hammering at the door, kicking it, hacking it, beating it with the bat, but they both knew that he would never get it open, and that they were both safe from the sum of his rage, and safe from facing each other. What would have happened if just once he had opened the door his brother thought would never give way?

He remembers other doors he's hidden behind, and doors that he's pounded on that remained closed. Perhaps it's doors like those that have drifted until they've gathered here: doors never opened, doors that remained mute and anonymous, doors slammed in faces, doors locked on secrets, and violated doors, doors stripped of their privacy—pried, jimmied, axed. If not for the crescendo of knocking, he might lean his ear to each door and hear its story, listen to the voices muffled behind it, the singing or laughter or cursing or weeping, and perhaps he would recognize voices, so that it would seem as if he were walking down a long corridor lined with all the doors of his life.

But by now the pounding has become too terrible for him to even consider listening for voices. It is a racket beyond control, rage or panic desperately unleashed, like someone beating at the lid of a coffin. He covers his ears. It seems impossible that the doors can continue to withstand such a battering. And if one of them should give—split by the fury of blows—would all the pressure from beneath come gushing through that single doorway, spouting like a monstrous wave into the sky, then storming down, crushing, drowning, sucking the surface under, leaving only the bobbing flotsam of shattered doors behind?

The vision terrifies him. He turns to run back across the doors, his footfalls drumming as he retraces his steps to the edge of the sea. Now it is as if all the various knocks have been reduced to a single, massive fist pounding as steady as a heartbeat against a single, massive door. Each concussion knocks him off his feet and sends him sprawling across the wooden surface. As he dreaded, he can hear the wood begin to splinter and a network of cracks spread as if it is ice rather than wood that he flees across.

At the edge of the doors, surf pounds in, in time to the pounding of the fist. The surge of breakers buckles his legs. He's rolled back across the doors, then, caught in the backwash, sucked out toward the sea until the next wave sweeps him back again. He manages to catch hold of a knocker and he clings to it while waves slam over his body. With his free hand and his teeth, he works to untie the knot to the line of the raft, while, at the other end of the line, the raft jerks and strains like a terrified dog at a leash. Finally the knot comes loose, and he times the backwash so that its momentum sweeps him into the raft. He's thrown in on his face, water piling onto his back, while the raft bucks wildly in the surf, spinning away from shore. At any moment he expects it to capsize.

He is on the sea, drifting once more toward the horizon, staring out into a monochromic blue, and not a bird in the sky. He paddles aimlessly, waiting for a current to seize the raft. Behind him, the doors gleam like a beach in the sun. They have fallen silent again. Whatever was awakened must be sinking back unanswered into dark fathoms. When he turns the raft for a final look, ripples slap the bow like the last reverberations of those desperate blows.

Hometown

Not everyone still has a place they've come from. So Martin tries to describe a single version of his multiple nowheres to a city girl one summer evening as they stroll past anonymous statues and the homeless camped like picnickers on lawns that momentarily look bronzed. The shouts of Spanish kids from the baseball diamond beyond the park lagoon reminds him of playing outfield for the hometown team. They played after the workday was over, by the mothy beams of tractors and combines, and the glow of an enormous harvest moon. At twilight you could see the seams of the moon more clearly than the seams of the ball. He can remember a home run sailing over his head into a cornfield, sending up a cloudburst of crows . . .

Later, heading with her toward a rented room in a transient hotel, past open bars, the smell of sweat and stale beer dissolves into a childhood odor of fermentation: the sour, abandoned granaries by the railroad tracks where the single spark from a match might still explode. A gang of boys would go there to smoke the pungent, impotent, homegrown weed and sometimes, they said, to meet a certain girl.

They never knew when she'd be there. Just before she appeared the whine of locusts became deafening and grasshoppers whirred through the shimmering air. The daylight moon suddenly grew near enough for them to see that it was filled with the reflection of their little fragment of the world, and then the gliding shadow of a hawk ignited an explosion of pigeons from the granary silos.

They said, beware, a crazy bum lived back there, too, but if so, Martin never saw him.

Ant

She was dozing on a faded Navajo blanket with the filmy shade of a maple tree drawn like a veil across her skin. Her blouse was still opened to where he'd unbuttoned it down to the sky-blue of the bra she'd brought back as a souvenir from Italy.

Rob was lying just beyond the edge of the shadows thrown by her eyelashes. He had removed his shirt and spread it beneath him on the grass. It was hot, and lounging in her company seemed to intensify the light. Even the birds were drowsy. Only a single ant was working. It had him by the toe.

"Trying to tow me away," he would have called out to her but for the lassitude, and her aversion to puns. The Woman Who Hates Puns, she sometimes called herself.

With his eyes closed and the sun warm on his lids, it seemed as if he and the ant were the only creatures on the planet still awake. At first, Rob was simply amused by its efforts, but after a while he began to sense a nearly imperceptible movement across the grass. He squinted up into the high blue sky, not caring really where he was headed. It was a day for such an attitude, but then almost any day spent with her could trigger a mood like that—could require it, in fact. Since he'd met her, Rob had increasingly spent his days in a trance for which he had no name. To describe this state of mind, he joked that he was living in Limbo.

This was Limbo: high, heavenly-looking clouds that threw

no shadow and assumed no shapes. No wind, yet a faint hiss in the trees. Sunlight faintly weighted with perfume. In Limbo, where dream ruled, siestas were mandatory. The grass slid gently beneath him without leaving a stain along his spine. Grass blades combed his hair as he went by until his hair assumed the slant of grass.

So long as it was only a single ant, Rob didn't mind. He wouldn't tolerate them marching up his body in black columns, swarming, entering his mouth, ears, nostrils, and eyes in a pulsing stream, as if he were just another corpse to clean.

It was a morbid vision, not in keeping with such a lovely day.

Even here in Limbo, Rob thought, one apparently never recovers from having had "Leiningen Versus the Ants" read to him as a child.

He could still remember his anticipation—a mix of excitement and terror—on those Sunday afternoons in summer when his uncle Wayne would arrive with a storybook under his arm. Uncle Wayne would come to babysit for little Robbie while Rob's parents went out to the backyard barbecues from which they would return "pickled," as his father called it— though they looked more as if they'd been boiled—smelling of Manhattans, and laughing too easily and loudly.

"Remember," his mother would caution conspiratorially before she left, "don't ask Uncle Wayne about the war. He doesn't like to talk about it. And don't worry if he doesn't talk much at all."

As young as Rob was, it was clear to him that the babysitting was as much for Uncle Wayne's sake as it was for the sake of Rob's parents or himself.

Uncle Wayne usually didn't talk much when his parents were there. He seemed shy, embarrassed, almost ashamed. His face was pitted from acne, which gave him the look of a teenager. Sometimes, Rob imagined that Uncle Wayne's face had been pitted by shrapnel.

"Do you like stories?" his uncle had asked him during their first visit.

"Sure," Rob said.

"Good. Stories are what kept me sane," Uncle Wayne said, then laughed in the odd, stifled way of his as if at a private joke between them.

But reading aloud, his uncle lost his shyness. Uncle Wayne didn't simply read stories, he lived them. During "The Most Dangerous Game," Rob had to run from room to room while his uncle, reading aloud the entire time, stalked him, the storybook in one hand, and in the other a bow made from a clothes hanger strung with a rubber band and armed with an arrow fashioned from a cardboard pant guard.

When they read "The Monkey's Paw," Rob hid behind his bedroom door while his uncle mounted the stairs with the heavy-footed, ominous tread of someone dead who'd been summoned back from the grave. Nearly quaking with fear, Rob had tried to wish him back into his grave while his uncle Wayne pounded on the door.

His uncle would open the book by Edgar Allan Poe and turn to his favorite story, "The Tell-Tale Heart," and the boy would force himself to watch his uncle's face so as not to miss the instantaneous transformation when his uncle's eyes assumed a maniacal gleam and his mouth twisted into a malevolent smile as he read the opening words: "True!—nervous—very, very dreadfully nervous I had been and am; but why *will* you say that I am mad?" And then he'd burst into a spit-flecked spasm of psychopathic laughter.

But of all the stories they read together, it was "Leiningen Versus the Ants" that was the most frightening and memorable. How many Sunday afternoons, while other boys watched double-headers or shot baskets at a hoop suspended above a carport, had Rob sat sweating and listening intently as Uncle Wayne read about Leiningen making his way through the jungle, evading the hordes of army ants?

The ants streamed past barriers of water and fire, relentlessly consuming everything in their path with their black grinding mandibles, mandibles that could strip a man down to his bones as neatly and savagely as a school of piranhas.

Rob ran from the ants through the house, pursued by his uncle, who was draped in a blanket that served as the amorphous shape of massing ants. Rob would race around the table with the ants gaining on him, knocking over chairs as they went. He'd gallop up the stairs with the ants at his heels, slam himself into his room, but the weight of the ants would force open the door. He'd jump on his bed with nowhere else to run or hide as the ants oozed over his feet and began to engulf him, while flushed and wild he'd beat at them with a pillow, tussling, wrestling, and finally, overpowered, nearly smothered by them, he'd have to scream, "Leiningen doesn't die! The ants don't get him! The ants don't win!"

Only then, reminded of the authority of the story, would his uncle sink back, his acne feverish, hands shaking, and silently they'd both return downstairs, which was where Rob's parents would find them, eating popsicles and watching the ball game, when they returned home.

Remembering his uncle, Rob had forgotten the ant. There was an obvious bad pun there at which The Woman Who Hates Puns would have groaned. But even had Rob said it aloud, she might not have heard him, for the ant had managed to work its way beneath Rob's back and, seizing his belt with its mandibles, had lifted him off the ground the merest fraction of a millimeter, balancing Rob so perfectly that neither his head nor heels dragged. And having succeeded in carrying Rob across the boundary of Limbo, back into the ordinary world, the ant now proceeded at a considerably more determined pace.

They went along like that, hurrying away from his slumbering Love, like a grain of rice from a wedding.

Ransom

Once, in college, broke and desperate, I kidnapped myself.

Ransom notes were sent to all interested parties. Later, I sent hair and fingernail clippings as well.

They steadfastly insisted on an ear.

Marvelous Encounters of My Life

"You're going to leave your watch on?" she'd asked as if it were an offense on the order of undressing down to all but his socks.

Had there been a teasing note in her voice?

Earlier in the evening, at the bar, on their third drink and discussing favorite films, she'd said that she loved Hollywood movies from the thirties and forties for the banter between men and women. Myrna Loy and William Powell in *The Thin Man*; Gable and Claudette Colbert in *It Happened One Night*; Cary Grant and Rosalind Russell in *His Girl Friday*; and, of course, Bogart and Bacall in *To Have and Have Not*, where Bacall delivers her famous zinger: "You know how to whistle, don't you, Steve? You just put your lips together and blow."

"The America the women and men in those black-and-white movies staked out between them seems so different from the here and now," she said, nostalgic for a time and country she never lived in.

"Different how?" he asked.

"Well, for starters, they meant something very different by *adult* entertainment. Movies today star cartoons. The culture's been totally infantilized."

Outside the bar, the thunderstorm that had made catching a cab impossible continued to rumble. Neither of them had an umbrella. His first sight of her face had been through the spattered glass panels of the revolving door she'd entered just before he did—both of them ducking out of the downpour into the hotel bar.

The bartender wore livery—white jacket, maroon bow tie. Behind the mahogany bar, a two-story slab of cobalt mirror reflected bolts of spring lightning. Three empty barstools away, her reflection sat sipping a flute of champagne. Instead of a beer, he ordered a martini, not a drink he ever drank alone, and between flashes of lightning sneaked glances at her until their eyes met in the mirror. She seemed about to smile before glancing down at the glass she was raising to her lips. It gave him the nerve to try starting a conversation.

Excuse me, he might say, *I couldn't help noticing that you celebrate rain, too.* That had the advantage of being true—he'd always loved the smell of rain—but as an ice-breaker, true or not, it sounded fake and nearly as precious as it would be to recite what he recalled from a poem about rain:

> *It's raining women's voices as if they'd died even*
>   *in memory,*
> *and it's raining you as well marvellous encounters*
>   *of my life . . .*

He didn't want the rain to let up.

What if he turned and said: *I was just sitting here thinking how I'd be willing to bet that in every life there must be at least one instance when fate came disguised as weather.*

"No umbrella, either?" he asked her. "I wonder if that makes us optimists?"

"Actually, I left mine on the train coming in," she said. "The hotel loans them out but I didn't think to take one. I'm not sure what that makes me. Distracted, maybe."

"The train from where?" he asked, rather than "Distracted by what?"

By last call they'd returned to the subject of umbrellas. She'd begun to touch him lightly, reflexively, as one might to make a point, while recounting the story of how, on her ninth birthday, when she asked her mother for a clear plastic umbrella so that she could watch the raindrops fall, her mother told her, "Clair, dear, you don't pay enough attention to where you're going as is, let alone without staring up into the clouds."

They were tipsy and laughing as they left the bar, not through the revolving door, but by a side exit that opened onto the hotel lobby.

And later in her room, maybe what she had actually asked was "Do you always leave your watch on?" That was a completely different kind of question—not banter. That was a question about history.

The watch was from the thirties, with a Deco rose-gold face and a genuine alligator band complete with a tiny rose-gold buckle. Despite her nostalgia for that era, it obviously had not occurred to her that such a watch could have played a supporting role in one of those movies she loved: Cary Grant might have worn it to check if Katharine Hepburn was running predictably late. It was the kind of vintage watch that people assume must have a family history, otherwise why would one go through the trouble of winding it each morning? He'd been asked more than once if the watch had a sentimental value—if it had been passed down to him from his father or maybe his grandfather. When she asked if he was leaving it on, he considered for a moment telling her that the watch had belonged to his father and was the whole of the inheritance his father had left him.

That would have been starting off (if this was the start of anything) with a lie, the kind of finagling tale his father was infamous for. His father, a gambler—he referred to himself as a *joueur*—was a man who, if going to the track was impossible, would settle for bingo. He was still alive, a little demented—or was that just drink—and living in a retirement community outside Vegas. He had visited his father there once and the place struck him as a subdivision gated not to keep the riffraff out, but to keep its population of bookies, hustlers, and scam artists in.

He had actually bought the watch in a secondhand shop after an acupuncture session with Dr. Wu had left him euphoric. Dr. Wu was treating his spring allergies, allergies he'd inherited from his father along with a tendency to squander money as well as his given name, Julian. Like his father, he went by Jules; neither he nor his father could tolerate "Junior." Dr. Wu's office was downtown, and after treatment Jules would find himself at some pricey men's store buying clothes he didn't need. Perhaps Dr. Wu, in collusion with local merchants, was inserting a needle in a point that triggered buying sprees. One particularly radiant afternoon, Jules walked through downtown crowds feeling as if the vital force, qi, were emanating from his body. He noticed that women, and men as well, glanced as he passed as if the force were visible to them, too. On Jewelers Row, under the L tracks, he stopped before a window where a watch with a face the color of rose champagne caught his eye. An L train reverberated overhead like a drumroll. Until that moment he'd never considered buying a vintage watch, but suddenly he had to have it. When he entered the shop, the immediately attentive saleswoman stared at him in the way that people on the street had stared, while he described the watch in the window. "Yes, sir," she said, "right away, sir," and rushed to get it. Not until he saw himself in the mirror on the counter did he realize that Dr. Wu, who only an hour earlier had inserted a four-inch needle in the Baihui point at the top of Jules's skull—a powerful point where all the yang energy of the body converges—had overlooked removing the needle, which was sticking from the top of his head like an antenna.

If Clair had noticed his watch in the bar, Jules would have told her how he had come to buy it, much as she had told him about the clear plastic umbrella. But now wasn't the time to launch into a story.

"You're going to leave your watch on?" she asked.

"You're leaving on your cross?"

The Samaritan

On a humid night when it's quiet enough after a rain to hear the drainpipes dripping into the alley, a voice—if a moan can be called a voice—passes like vapor through the rain-plugged window screen. It's only another night noise at first, inseparable from the static that passes for silence in a city—traffic, insects, nighthawks, leaking rain gutters, someone doors away playing a radio or practicing on a cello. But gradually the moan grows more insistent. There's a rhythm to it that Marty begins to detect, a resonance in its tail of ragged breathing—and out of a half sleep Marty's eyes open, alert in the dark, and he listens, alarmed.

Someone is hurt, the victim of a hit-and-run or a rape or a mugging, or someone is sick, or perhaps grieving, expressing each throb of a wound—a muffled, irrepressible cry, the mouthing of a single, aching, mournful vowel. Alarm is his first reaction and his second is a kind of paralysis, as he lies listening, realizing that if someone is hurt, it's his responsibility to help. He doesn't want to think of himself as one of those alienated people in cities who will trade off their humanity rather than risk getting involved. He needs to do something, at least to inquire if help is needed—a stranger coming to the aid of a stranger. Or could he be sued for trying to help? Maybe he should simply call 911 and let them handle it. But if he called, what would he tell them? *Help, I think I hear someone moaning.*

By now, Marty is totally awake, sweating, staring into the dark, straining to hear every nuance of the sound. It's a woman's voice. He's sure of that. The moans have become steady, there's almost a singsong about them, and something else—a throatiness that makes each moan more disorientingly familiar than the last, as if he's gone from a hypnagogic dream directly to a déjà vu. Suppose it's an auditory hallucination. But the longer Marty strains to listen, the more convinced he becomes that he is hearing the voice of the woman in the apartment one floor down from his, the shy-looking one who wears a Dodgers cap when she jogs—maybe she moved here from L.A.—the girl downstairs who would rather look away than nod hello, even though one day Marty went to the trouble of buying a Cubs hat and timing his trip to the mailbox in the lobby so as to be there when she came jogging in, her hair a little sweaty, her face flushed and more full of life than usual. He'd hoped that maybe the baseball hats would give them something to talk about, but she didn't notice and jogged past him before he could say, *How 'bout them Dodgers*, or whatever he was going to say. He'd never rehearsed the exact words, just hoped that at the time he'd say something right, but she didn't notice him any more than she seems to notice how alone she appears. It's only the sound of her moaning that carries from her bedroom window a floor below, moaning in a steady chant which she can't know has disturbed him. Like a voice crying alone in the wilderness, Marty thinks, and yet she'd be mortified to know he's overheard her. He'll never tell. It's a secret he'll keep safe from a world of predators. Everything's all right, it's none of his business, after all, he can simply lie back now, relax, and close his eyes, listening as her breath grows rapid, wilder, rises an octave then plunges to a guttural sigh—a sigh to which, tonight, he tries to time his own moan—before they both drop off to sleep.

Fantasy

"Do you fantasize about me?" she asked.

"Sure," he said, not volunteering any more information.

"I have the oddest fantasies about what I'd like to do with you," she said.

"Like what, for instance?"

"I want to shave you."

"I want to shave you, too," he said.

"Not that way," she said. "I mean it. I picture you soaking in a steamy tub, a beautiful old claw-footer, and I lather your beard with a boar-bristle brush. I even know where they sell them—at Crabtree and Evelyn. Then you lie back and close your eyes, and with an old-fashioned straight razor that makes the sexiest scraping sound, I give you the best, closest shave you'll ever have. Shave you clean and smooth and rinse your skin as if I'm your geisha."

"Sounds nice," he said, rather than tell her there was no way in hell she was getting near him with a razor.

Transaction

"I wouldn't mind selling my body if somebody'd offer to buy."

"You're kidding," George said.

"Actually, George, it's not an especially original female fantasy. But besides the fantasy turn-on, there's something attractively up-front about it. A simple transaction seems honest compared to the bullshit I've seen that passes for a quote 'relationship' between men and women."

George raised his coffee cup and sipped. The pause was a part of a conversation in which he was at a momentary loss for words. From across the green Formica table of their vinyl booth, he eyed Britt skeptically. "How much would you charge?"

"How much do you have?"

"What do you mean?"

"What do you mean, 'what do you mean'? It wasn't a rhetorical question, George. How much do you have on you?"

George shrugged, then made a show of checking. He put his ballpoint pen, cell phone, and key ring on the table in order to do a thorough job of searching his pockets. "Thirty-two dollars and thirteen cents, and I have to pay for lunch."

"You can put lunch on plastic. Me, it's cash only."

"You wouldn't take a personal check from someone you know?"

"George, you're married. To a lawyer. You're my supervisor, we shouldn't even be having lunch, and you're talking about leaving a paper trail. Cold hard cash."

"So, what would thirty-two thirteen buy?"

"I'm open to negotiation. The ball's in your court, George."

He seemed at a loss for words again, outflanked, clearly surprised, though still capable of sneaking an appraising look at Britt as if she'd been suddenly transformed from a receptionist in a gray pantsuit to a courtesan dressed for evening. She winked and brushed his ankle under the table with the toe of her shoe.

"You've got to get into the spirit of this to take it further, George," she said, dropping her voice. "My just telling you in plain English what's possible will cost something. Per word. Sorry if that sounds mercenary, but that's the culture we live in. The more explicit I am—per word—the more expensive just listening will be, and the less you'll have to spend on the very things being discussed. If you can't think of something to ask for, tell me a fantasy. I already told you one of mine."

"I never called one of those phone-sex numbers or anything like that," George said. "Some people are naturally verbal. I don't think I could say anything straight out. How did we even get on this subject?"

"As I recall, I asked why you always spend lunch with a spy novel, and you explained that spy novels aren't so much about plot twists as they are about alienation, and from there you started talking about the deception and loneliness of the average daily life."

"Exactly right," George said.

"And somehow you jumped from that into how you didn't understand how loneliness could send a man to a prostitute, as afterward he'd only be lonelier. Frankly, George, that sounds to me like you've been entertaining the thought of a little covert action. Here. If you can't say your secret desires aloud, then write." She stripped a napkin from the dispenser on the table and pushed it over to him.

He smiled and shook his head as if surrendering to her comical ingenuity. Instead of writing, he clicked his ballpoint pen and drew a stick figure: round head, two arms and legs, then added a stick erection.

"Is that drawn to scale?" Britt asked.

He started again: a new stick figure, this one minus the erection but wearing a top hat.

"Why not give him a cane, too? What do we have here—you and your shadow strolling down the avenue? Which of those is you, George, and which one is George's evil twin?"

"Maybe this is the covert Fred Astaire–me," George said.

"I don't do twins," she said. "Too kinky. No threesomes. You could have thirty-two *thousand* dollars and thirteen cents and it wouldn't be enough for a group rate, George."

"I wasn't suggesting anything of the kind," George said, then added quietly, "I'd want you to myself." He crossed out the two stick men on the napkin and drew another. To indicate gender, instead of an erection or a hat, he added antlers.

"No animals, either," Britt said. "Or is that a shaman? No shamans. For God's sake, no wonder you were afraid to say these things aloud. Orgies, gangbangs, bestiality, human sacrifice. We're talking about a crummy thirty-two dollars and thirteen stinking cents here, George. Unlike love, the art of negotiation takes place at the intersection of realistic expectations."

"According to whom?"

"I think Gandhi said that, George."

He turned the napkin over and drew a stick figure with a circle head, on which he sketched hair meant to mimic Britt's moussed spiky hairstyle. He added Orphan Annie eyes, a big happy smile, and two tiny circles punctuated with periods for breasts. The figure, wearing high heels à la Minnie Mouse, stood with legs akimbo. At the V of her stick legs he scribbled in pubic hair.

"George, the sixties bush is out."

He ignored her comment and drew an unadorned stick man kneeling before the female figure, with his oval head seemingly pressed to her scraggly crotch. "It was the word 'intersection.' I'm very impressionable," he explained apologetically.

Britt blushed, then tried to grab the napkin. "It's for my Great Moments scrapbook," she said.

George managed to crush it up first. He stuffed it in his shirt pocket. "No paper trail," he told her.

The waitress came by. "Everything okay? Dessert?" she asked.

"Just the bill, please," George said, glancing at his watch.

The waitress set the bill on the table and George placed his credit card on top of it without bothering to check the amount.

"You pay at the cashier," the waitress said, "but I'll take it up for you if you want."

"No, that's okay," George said.

"It's no problem," the waitress said.

"I'll follow protocol," George said. "I'll put the tip on the credit card."

"More coffee?" the waitress asked.

"We're good, thank you," George said.

After the waitress walked off, George put his key ring, cell phone, and ballpoint pen back in his pockets and slid the coffee cups and water glasses to the side with the salt and pepper shakers so that the stretch of table between him and Britt was clear.

"I'm sure she'd rather have the tip in cash, then you don't have to report it," he said. He wiped the trail that the water glasses left on the Formica with a napkin, then folded the wet napkin and placed it on top of the napkin dispenser. She silently watched him tidying up.

"You don't have to tell me—I know I'm anal," George said.

"Not for thirty-two thirteen you're not."

He stacked the money, the coins on top of the bills—it looked like a sizable tip—then slid it across the table. Britt didn't reach for it. She remained seated, looking at the money piled before her.

"The ball's in your court now," George said.

"You want to see me take it, don't you? That's a turn-on. What if I don't touch it? Just leave it between us? Would you pick it back up?"

George said nothing.

"Don't worry, I won't put you in that position."

She lifted her purse from the seat, a pink-striped blue straw bag stuffed with her gym shoes, opened it at the edge of the table, and, as one might brush off crumbs, scooped the bills and change from the Formica into her purse.

"Did you like that?"

"It should be more," George said.

"No problem. I'm making eighteen an hour to sit behind a desk all day. This is a significant raise." She dug out a disposable lighter and a pack of Virginia Slims and stood. "I'll be outside giving myself cancer," she said. "Don't forget John le Carré."

George picked up his book, paid the cashier with his credit card, and went outside.

Britt was leaning against the brick wall, smoking.

"That money's yours, no strings attached," George said. "I know being a single mother's no picnic. My mom raised me and my sister after our old man ran out on us."

"Do you think that was about charity for either of us, George? I'd offer a receipt, but no paper trail," she said.

"I don't need one," George said. "I'll remember everything about it."

"I'm glad you'll get your money's worth."

Flu

Faye's illness transformed her in a way no diet or face-lift could have. After days of nausea, vertigo, diarrhea; a fast of toast and tea; fever; dreams that came and went more like mirages; an aching lethargy that demanded fourteen-hour sleeping spells from which she'd wake confused but only too aware of how terribly alone she was, Faye felt better.

The usual grim weariness was gone from around her lips. Her eyes no longer peered out like a miner's from sallow tunnels smudged with mascara. They seemed enlarged with light, glowing limpidly from her pale face. Even the shadow beneath her chin where her darkness most accumulated had burned away. It was as if everything unessential had burned away.

"What happened to you?" Aldo blurted, startled by the sight of her sitting, legs crossed, back behind the reception desk.

"Flu," Faye said. "Everybody's getting it. I mean, you sit up here in front all day and you're going to come in contact with everything anybody walks in with."

"Everybody should get so sick," Aldo said.

It seemed to Faye an odd remark at the time, but she ignored it and kept talking, about the job, the weather, the flu epidemic. It was the first conversation she'd had since she'd been sick and she clung to it, needing desperately to talk, aware the entire time of how Aldo was watching her.

And later, when people would ask them how they met and fell in love, it was always Aldo who would answer. "Flu." He'd smile earnestly. "It all started with flu. I still haven't recovered."

Swing

The mute boy was dragging the great stalled clock from his father's study to the trash heap that smoldered at the edge of the woods when an old man with a stick chased him.

Back when the boy's father was alive, he'd tried to console his son, and maybe himself as well, by telling him that, in ways mysterious, God always compensates. In place of speech, God must have given the boy some gift—perhaps a rare gift of the spirit, one the boy would recognize only when he grew older. His father was mistaken, not about there being a gift but about when the boy would recognize it, for even as a child he knew his compensation for silence was speed—winged heels. The boy believed that he was fast enough to outrun everyone, any danger, too fast to be overtaken even by the stride of the stilt-legged shadow of Death. But he kept this a secret from everyone, including his father, because he was afraid his father would be disappointed. Speed wasn't a rare spiritual gift. He didn't reveal it even when, to the resounding, impassive tick of the study clock, his father lay weeping on his deathbed. His father wept because he was leaving his dumb son with a stepmother who cared more for her ferret than him, and with the stepmother's bitter twin sister, who, expelled from the convent, paced the halls of the mansion at night moaning her beads and tearing at her newly grown-out hair.

The boy kept his secret until the old man with the stick

came after him. The old man swung the stick in an arc that would have dislodged the boy's head had he not ducked and darted away. He could hear the whine of air swatted behind him as the old man pursued him. The man might have been old and his trousers droopy, but he ran surprisingly well, and the longer he chased, the more determined he seemed to catch the boy. They were racing along a puddled forest path strewn with deadfall and, afraid he'd trip, the boy didn't dare look back. The rush of his running drew the skin tight over his face, as if he were masked in latex. As he ran the boy unclasped a silver penknife that had belonged to his father and butchered his unkempt hair so that it no longer streamed behind him, snagging on the branches that shredded his clothes. To protect his eyes from the pressure of velocity and from the blurred birches with their slashing limbs, the boy kept his gaze on the earth scrolling beneath his feet.

He could outpace the flailing stick that had elongated into a hooked bone, he could outdistance the shouts of the old man's threats and curses, the baying of the greyhounds the old man had summoned, the shadow of the falcon he'd released; he could leave his own fear behind, though to do so required that the boy outrun everything he knew—every memory, every dream, every thought, every emotion, all burning off like the tail of the icy comet that was his past. He ran in the vacuum of his own momentum, a stitch splitting his side as he threatened to outrun his own breath. It was then he realized, in a way that would have pleased his father, that such impossible running could only be a rare gift of the spirit.

When he came upon the swing in a glade that opened like a neglected garden at the heart of the forest, he finally stopped. He waded into sunlight as if it were a pool. Scarred by thorns, his outgrown clothes reduced to rags, the boy stood half immersed in the solemn shafts streaming through a canopy of green. He felt overwhelmed by an emptiness that never would have caught him had he continued running. He knew he couldn't retrace his steps and retrieve all he had discarded; except for the silver penknife, the past was lost. But as the whistle of velocity echoing in his ears dissolved into silence, and the silence dissolved into birdsong, toad-trill, insect-drone, the boy gradually became aware that in his blur of acceleration he had learned about the forest—its birds, berries, mushrooms, roots. Instinctively, he had given them all names, and in order to do so, he had created a lexicon. Perhaps he'd been mute because he'd been born into the wrong language, into a tongue with unspeakable words. Now he possessed a language he could speak, one he could sing, if only there was someone to listen.

He imagined that somewhere else on earth people were conversing in the language he had created.

The boy sat on the weathered swing that dangled at the center of the glade like an amulet the forest wore. It rocked of its own accord—a rowboat riding gentle swells, a pendulum that would ticktock for infinity now that someone had nudged it into motion. The soles of his shoes, near worn away from running, brushed over the weeds and hissed a breeze. He unclasped the penknife to dig his initials into the wooden seat, but he couldn't recall them. A memory found its way back to him, of a day at the park with his father. His father had lifted him into a baby swing and carefully secured him with a bar that fit across his lap—it prevented accidents but also escape. Having secured his son, his father seemed to lose control. The boy couldn't see his father's uncharacteristic glee, but he heard him laughing each time he pushed from behind. His father swung him gently at first, then gradually higher and higher until the boy's mouth gaped open in a mute scream, a scream his father could not hear. He was pushing so wildly that the swing careened and its chains twisted, and the boy imagined they might snap. Between convulsions of his father's hilarity, the boy heard a nurse, who was pushing an elderly lady in a wheelchair, exclaim: "Oh, Lordy! Look at that crazy white man flingin' that boy!"

If his father heard the comment, he ignored her, and continued flinging him up until, dizzy, the boy could hear an otherworldly vibration—solar wind, the music of the spheres, seraphim—whatever it was, its dissonance was terrifying.

Later, as they walked home hand in hand, his father asked if he'd glimpsed the angels who played their harps on clouds, and the boy shook his head no, a moment of defiance for which he now, at least in memory, felt petty and ashamed.

Oh, Lordy! This was no baby swing he was riding. He swung earnestly now, easily pumping over the trees. He swung in a straight arc to a steady rhythm, and the memory of his father vanished. He no longer needed its companionship, no longer felt empty and alone. It was as if he and the swing, sharing a single passion, were becoming one. Each pump of his body carried them farther into blue sky. The wind of his swinging gusted blossoms from orchards and parted fields of grain below. If I were a girl, he thought, I'd look up her blowing dress. He gripped the ropes as gently as he might the braids of a girl. Still, his palms grew callused. He swung standing, kneeling, sitting; at night, he slept oscillating beneath the whorled Milky Way and dreamed of traversing luminous oceans that rose and fell in time to the gravity of the swing. Each morning he woke to find the swing had taken them farther than the day before.

Perhaps he would have remained one with the swing, and be swinging still, if not for the day when he heard a name being called in the language that he'd learned as he ran through the forest. A name—his name?—was being called out over and over. He listened and couldn't be sure. When he called back, frayed tendrils sprouted from the swing's ropes and vined his wrists, arms, and chest, coiling at his throat and choking off his voice. He swung as if caught in the rigging of a ship, but he managed to pry open his father's penknife and cut himself loose before a violent backswing shook the knife from his hand. On the upswing, he let go.

Think of dreams in which you fly. By which you fly.

How does it happen?

Sometimes, I fly unaided, as if flight were natural, although even in the dream I know it's not. I'll be running hurdles on a dark track like the one I'd train on alone at night in high school after the stadium gate was locked at ten p.m. I'd scale the cyclone fence to sneak in, and then lug the hurdles onto the track from where they'd been stacked along the sidelines. They weren't modern aluminum hurdles, but old-style heavy wooden ones that bruised your knee when you clipped them, if you were lucky enough not to have your legs knocked out from under you. In those days of cinder tracks, athletes wore spikes gracile like ballet shoes. The spikes made you run on the balls of your feet, almost up on your toes; just tying them on made me feel lighter and faster, as if I were attaching winged heels. I'm wearing spikes in my dream, so maybe I don't fly unaided after all. A friend once told me she had a dream in which she could fly after lacing on red ice skates, and that while she skated ecstatically over the rooftops, her mother kept shouting from below, "You be careful, young lady, you're skating on thin air!"

There are three strides between each hurdle if you run them right, but in my dream, all I need is a single stride before I'm skimming the next hurdle. And then I realize I don't need to touch down at all. I can glide from hurdle to hurdle, and gliding becomes flight.

It's always night in my flying dreams. Sometimes, I fly unaided, or relatively so, but other times there are conveyances:

a kite that pulls me up as it rises, a unicycle on which learning to balance becomes learning to levitate, an anti-gravity air taxi shaped vaguely like an inflatable life raft that hovers at my fifth-floor window while I climb aboard. A crew not unlike the Marx Brothers pilots it. Their names are Rosco, Bosco, and Moscow.

A woman once told me of a dream in which her blue Toyota was able to fly. The Toyota was the first car she'd bought herself, after graduating from college, with money from her first real job.

"Was it night when you could fly?" I asked, envisioning the taillights of her Toyota firing like rockets while her radio blared Prince's "Little Red Corvette."

"You mean like a witch with her broom? No, I was driving down a two-lane past fields Technicolor with wheat, and green pastures where horses grazed. It was bright! I was wearing sunglasses, and had the windows down, and the car filled with the smell of fields and horses. A breeze that looked so gentle combing through the wheat whipped in, blowing my hair, and I noticed that on the other side of the barbed-wire fence the horses were racing my car. Their manes and tails streamed, and I realized I was seeing them from above. I could see the shadow of my Toyota gliding among the horses, sailing off with the herd across the pasture, and that's when I knew I was flying. It was so free, beautiful, like being able to do anything. It wasn't a sex dream, but it felt physical, almost climactic. When I woke I thought about it all day, carried it with me like a secret. I could still feel that buoyancy, and when the feeling began to slip away I knew I didn't want to live without it and would do what I had to do so as to keep it. A week later I moved out on my husband and filed for a divorce and . . . and here we are playing hooky, having a drink," she said.

"I never had a flying dream like that," I told her, "one where I wake and know it's an omen."

"How can a flying dream not be an omen? What could it mean but that you could be untethered, free of all that's holding you down, holding you back? The gift is yours to accept, you have the power if you're willing to exercise it."

"I don't know," I said. "Freud says dreams are wishes, and who doesn't sometimes wish to fly? A wish is just a wish, it doesn't have to be unriddled like an omen or have a moral like a fable. Flying doesn't necessarily have to have a meaning. A bird doesn't have to analyze why he flies."

"What makes you think that what's apt for birds applies to you? Flying's natural for birds."

"Sometimes it feels almost natural," I said.

"Natural?" she scoffed. "Must be those inconspicuous wings of yours."

"If it's completely unnatural then we're back to witches and brooms—deals with the devil, not to mention Icarus and all the other myths that warn against defying nature and the gods."

"How do you feel when you fly?" she asked.

"Wonderful. Free, joyful."

"Ecstatic?"

"Sure, sometimes."

"You call feeling that way *natural*?" she asked. "What world are you living in? The ecstatic is by nature unnatural."

I laughed, not just at her cynicism but also at her deadpan delivery.

She stared back silently, and then said, "In my favorite novel, *The Great Gatsby*, Nick recalls a moment when it was as if he and Gatsby were in ecstatic cahoots. Ecstatic cahoots, the way we are sometimes, moment by moment. What kind of dream do you have to have to know when you've met someone you should change your life for?"

Here, on the island, *yesterday* and *tomorrow* are the same word. It's a language of inflection that's spoken—punctuated by sighs, lisps, growls, consonants suddenly expelled, vowels swallowed back into the shadow of a throat. On this coast of platinum sand, ravens have interbred with gulls. They perch on the horizon, disrupting the border between sea and sky. The elocution of birds echoes through the nacre vaults and conch cathedrals that litter a shoreline, along which he finds himself wading among schools of candlefish at an hour when the sun is setting. Or is it rising? Here, the word for sunset and sunrise is the same.

Midday. He hikes the hill path through the lemon groves. A snake slithering into shadow inscribes in cursive an undecipherable message in the dust. Ravens, gowned for graduation, take flight, and he pauses before the tire track he'd caught them studying, a staff on which white stones are arranged like notes. A melody he'd hum if he could read music.

Later, in a tiled courtyard called Palm Passage, he sits at a café table, sipping rum mixed with iced espresso. If he still had his father's penknife, he'd carve his name on the green coconut that has rolled beneath his chair—or, if not his name, then the name he heard them calling while he swung, a name he's since assumed.

Instead, he writes a letter. It's unaddressed. Are letters to no one inescapably written to oneself? To the self yet to be?

Those questions are how the letter opens. A chameleon skitters over the page and stops to do push-ups. They're part of the letter. Caught in a sudden updraft, hibiscus blossoms tumble across the tabletop. They're part of the letter, too, as are the rustling shadows of palms. As is what's missing—the accents he fails to mark, diacritical marks that should hover above each sentence like birds above a horizon. The language here is inflected even when written down, a language he invented but cannot control. It has assumed a life of its own.

He'll weight the page with a tip in foreign coins whose worth he's still not sure of, and leave what he's written for the rain to punctuate. The tip is for the young waitress with the sweating pitcher. Each time she leaned over the table to fill his water glass, her breasts, loose in a scooped-neck white dress, were revealed. When she caught him looking away, she smiled, her amused eyes a match for the sea beyond the platinum sand. He suspects that, like him, she's a stranger here.

Beyond the bird-flocked horizon, distant thunder grumbles, but in Palm Passage it appears as if there's already been a tropical downpour. The tiles are puddled where he surreptitiously emptied the water glass that she repeatedly filled. How thirsty he must have seemed. He's memorized her small nipples, nipples the reddish shade of bricks, and filed them carefully among a short inventory of secret glimpses: the breasts of singing mermaids that flashed like fish scales as he swung over the sea, the blur of the bathing nymphs he ran past in the forest long ago, the shadowy, plum-dark nipples of his stepaunt, who walked the clock-resounding, candlelit corridors in a muslin chemise, murmuring aves. Her hair, shorn in the convent, was growing out.

How does a woman come to renounce her beauty?

He remembers thinking, If I were a girl, I'd look up her blowing dress. The thunder rumbles closer, and he remembers the exhilaration of swinging through the rain.

She brings the letter to his room as if she's come to deliver it. Sunset/sunrise rays through the louvers. The hazy shadow of the overhead fan makes her white dress appear to whirl slowly.

She says, " 'It's raining hibiscus,' " and he's not sure how to respond. " 'Head full of light and rum,' " she says, " 'beneath the shadows of palms I was feeling ecstatic over nothing.' " She isn't speaking, but reading aloud, quoting the letter. " 'Eyes blue-green as sea, and nipples—what is the color of sunlight on bricks?' "

It's not what he remembers writing, but he doesn't deny

it. It's what he might have written, what he wanted to write. The language with a life of its own is rewriting the letter, rewriting the story of his life. It's a landscape of inflection they inhabit, a mercurial trill of echo and shadow, the accents traced along the spine with a fingernail as the words are whispered against an ear. At the eye of a private hurricane, an overhead fan draws her white dress over her head. Oh, Lordy, they begin to swing, a rhythmic momentum passing between them that threatens to fly out of control, and when she kneels, he clutches her hair, divides it into braids, and, in the whirring silence, holds on.

Between

guilt and desire, thought and act, *déjà* and *vu*, between
ampersand and cross, wing and air, all she made possible and
all she made impossible, between river and eel, loving and
leaving—a life like the exhalation that separates wine
and whine—between mute and mime, between the rhyme of
night and light, dream and waking from a nap in the afternoon darkness of what could have been a total eclipse but actually was an April thunderstorm, I thought the sound of men
lifting long lengths of rain gutter from a pickup truck was
a meteor shower rattling against the metal awning over Sun's
Oriental Food Store.

Arf

You ever had a boyfriend kissing your booty?

Girl, I never had no boyfriend who wasn't kissing my butt.

No, girl, I mean really kissing it.

Yeah, well, men are dogs. They want a sniff.

Kissing it all over.

Pass me that catsup.

All over. Like French kissing, you know what I'm saying? I got to spell it out for you, girl?

You the one bringing it up. At the dinner table.

I'm just curious to know you ever had a boyfriend like that? And this is coffee break not no dinner, for some of us at least.

Was a manner of speaking. We at a table. How's your catsup technique? I hate when it's a new bottle. One good splat and your food is like road-killed.

I got to go make a call. See you, girl. Them nasty jumbo fries gonna give you a jumbo booty.

Toujours pour la première fois
C'est à peine si je te connais de vue . . .

Professor Martino has written on a napkin: *Always for the first time, I scarcely know you when I see you.* The lines are by a French poet, but, Professor Martino thinks, Cole Porter might have written them. It is Martino's practice when traveling to a foreign country to bring a book of poems and a dictionary in the language of that place. He sits in an orange plastic booth, drinking black coffee, with still three more hours to kill before a flight to Paris. He allows himself to regress in airports to the diet of a kid—cinnamon buns, caramel corn, soft-serve. He's eaten the one Big Mac he'll eat this year, while imagining the bistro food to come—Belon oysters, rabbit with green olives, champagne—and thinking about the woman with whom he hopes to share those meals. They are supposed to meet at a boutique hotel on the river near Saint Germain, and he can't help worrying whether, even though it's a hotel she has chosen, she'll be there. He can't help wondering, though it is none of his business, what excuse she's made for the trip to her husband, whom she refers to by profession rather than name— the Frackologist.

Why stay with him? Professor Martino once asked.

Why do you think? she asked back, knowing he wouldn't answer.

Ma femme à la chevelure de feu de bois
Aux pensées d'éclairs de chaleur . . .

The dictionary has *femme* as woman or wife; the translation has it as wife: *My wife whose hair is a wood fire. Whose thoughts are heat lightning . . .*
Martin prefers *my woman.*

Ma femme aux cils de bâtons d'écriture d'enfant . . .
My woman whose eyelashes are strokes of a child's
writing . . .

Cole Porter wouldn't have come up with that.

The Frackologist is an executive with Halliburton who, she says, drank himself into a coronary before he became a cycling fanatic. He cycles on a recumbent bike before a wide-screen plasma television while watching classic boxing and at the end of his ride is soaked in sweat and panting like a dog.

My woman with buttocks of a swan's back
With buttocks of spring
And the sex of a gladiola . . .

Professor Martino is no longer consulting his French dictionary or writing lines on a napkin as if he is translating from scratch—he'll do better with the menu in Paris—for now he reads in English: *My woman with eyes of water to drink in prisons . . .*

Panting like a dog, giving me those cocker-spaniel eyes, sniffing around me like a dog in heat are the ways she's described the Frackologist. And, while Professor Martino has never heard her say men are dogs, when he catches the phrase from the booth behind him, he has an urge to turn, but doesn't. He never gets a look at the woman whose boyfriend likes to root around, but after she leaves, Professor Martino hears her friend, the woman with the fries, shake the crushed ice in her cup, take a slurp of her drink, and then whisper aloud, "Whore."

Fingerprints

Down at the 43rd Precinct they know that fingerprints don't
lie. The detectives study the inky orbits their coffee cups stamp
on blotters. They've seen it all. What's loneliness compared to
Missing Persons? Longing next to grand larceny? Love beside
assault with a deadly weapon?

But even the clerks know that crimes of passion leave clues.
Around midnight the report comes down from the boys in the
lab: your fingerprints are everywhere—on doorknobs, glasses,
mirrors, the shower stall, on the desktop when the lamp is lit,
on the silent, cradled telephone, on the sleeping screen, and
the keyboard—on each letter of the alphabet—on both sides
of windowpanes among old prints of rain. It's as if you needed
to touch everything. Or maybe you were just being careless
as usual, expecting, as usual, that we'll all simply keep letting
you go.

Mole Man

Her voice in the dark distilled his name down to a vowel until all that was left of it was breath shuddering over her teeth. He slid from her and they lay side by side without speaking.

"Sweetheart, I love your moans," he whispered.

In the stillness of the silenced window fan he listened to her breathing evenly again, and wondered if she'd heard what he'd just told her or if she was already adrift in sleep.

"That's good," she answered, "I'm covered with them."

"Covered with moans. That's nice. Baby, you're waxing poetic," he said.

"Moans?" she asked. "I thought you said *moles*."

"You thought I just told you that I love your moles?"

"It did sound a little odd," she said, "but I figured, well, if that's what he likes about me, fine."

"That has to be a first. I bet no one's used that line on you before?"

"Is that a rhetorical question?" she asked.

"I guess. I hope that at least you didn't imagine I was talking about those little myopic rodents tunneling in the dark through your front lawn even as we speak."

"Don't worry, sweetheart. The front lawn is Astroturf. And of course I thought you were referring to the moles on my skin."

"You were probably lying there thinking, dear Lord, there

are leg-men and tit-men and booty-men and neck-men—a nation of men in Japan worshipping pinups of Audrey Hepburn's neck—and hand-men and foot-men, as opposed to *a* footman, and no doubt shoulder-men and elbow-men and underarm-men and eye-, ear-, and nose-men, but I had to get involved with a mole-man?"

"Another rhetorical question?"

"It's too long to be rhetorical," he said.

"Then going back to your shorter rhetorical question about whether it's a first? For *me* yes, but I had a friend, Diane, who had a spray of strawberry moles on her stomach that she was self-conscious about. She had a fling with a guy named Hunter, an art student who claimed he could paint dreams. He loved kissing her moles, which she'd only let him do in the dark. One night on hashish she asks what exactly about her moles attracts him, and Hunter tells her he believes that, if connected, her moles will spell out the secret name of her soul mate, or maybe even his still-hidden face. So, stoned, she agrees to let him connect her moles. By the light of a flickering candle he draws lines along her skin. When he's finished, she winds herself in the sheet and stands before her mirror; he switches on the bed lamp and she opens the sheet. There's no name, no face. Only lines scribbled across her stomach attached to what looks like random punctuation. She feels utterly foolish. I need to take a shower, she says, but he begs, Please come with me, and drags her into the backyard, him in jockey shorts, her in the sheet. The summer sky is full of stars. He points—There's Betelgeuse, there's Rigel. He's obviously an amateur astronomer. He unwinds her sheet, spreads it on the grass, and she lies naked beneath the Milky Way while he compares the constellations to the moles connected on her stomach. It's Orion the Hunter, he says. You know the myth? Orion was killed by an arrow shot by Artemis—the Romans called her Diana, the goddess of the hunt, whom Orion adored.

Artemis placed his body in the night sky. You're wearing Orion's belt of stars."

"Sweetheart, that is one weird story. Love *is* strange. So, what happened to Hunter and Diane?" he asked.

"They broke up after Diane had a dermabrasion. See, when it comes to loving moles, I don't think it would be fair to categorize you as a mole-man. The bar for that is set too high."

"What category do I fall into?"

"You're more of a generalist," she said. "Moles just happen to be included."

"Every last one of them."

Bruise

She came over wearing a man's white shirt, rolled up at the sleeves, and a faded blue denim jumper that made her eyes appear more blue.

"Look," she said, sitting down on the couch and slowly raising the jumper, revealing a bruise high on the outside of her thigh.

It was summer. Bearded painters in spattered coveralls were painting the outside of the house white. Through the open windows they could hear the painters scraping the old, flaking paint from the siding on one side of the house, and the slap of paint-soaked brushes on the other.

"These old boards really suck up the paint," one of the painters would remark from time to time.

"I've always bruised so easily," she said, lowering her voice as if the painters might hear.

The bruise looked blue underneath the tan mesh of nylon. It was just off the hip, and above it he could see the lacy band of her panties. It was a hot day, climbing toward ninety, and as he studied the spot that she held her dress up for him to see, it occurred to him that even at this moment, it still might be possible for them to talk in a way that wasn't charged with secret meanings. Not every day needed to be imprinted on their memories. The direction their lives seemed, uncontrollably, to be taking might be changed, not by some revelation but in the course of an ordinary conversation, by the twist of a wisecrack or a joke, or perhaps by a simple question. He might ask why she was wearing pantyhose on such a hot day. Was it that her legs weren't tanned yet? He might rise from the couch and ask if she would like a lemonade, and when she said yes, he would go to the kitchen and make it—a real lemonade squeezed from the lemons in his refrigerator, their cold juice stirred with sugar and water, the granulated sugar whispering amid the ice, the ice cubes in a sweating glass pitcher clunking like a temple bell.

They could sit, sipping from cool glasses and talking about something as uncomplicated as weather, gabbing like painters, not because they lacked for more interesting things to talk about, but because it was summer and hot and she seemed not to have dressed for the heat.

Instead, when she crossed her legs in a way that hiked her dress higher and moved her body toward him, he touched the bruise with his fingertip, and pressed it more carefully and gently than one might jab at an elevator button.

Oh, her lips formed, though she didn't quite say it. She exhaled, closing her blue eyes, then opening them wider, almost in surprise, and stared at him. They were sitting very close together, their faces almost touching.

When he took his finger away she stretched the nylon over the bruise so he could better see its different gradations of blue. A pale green sheen surrounded it like an aura; purple capillaries ran off in all directions like tiny cracks, like a network of rivers on a map; there was violet at its center like a stain.

"It's ugly, isn't it?" she asked in a whisper.

He didn't answer, but pressed it again, slowly, deeply, and her head tilted back against a cushion. This time the *Oh* of her lips was audible. She closed her eyes and moaned, uncrossing her legs. They were sitting so close together that the sound of her nails scraping along nylon seemed to him almost a clatter the painters would hear. Her legs opened and he placed his palm against her and felt through the nylon heat, actual heat, like summer through a screen door.

He pressed the bruise again and again. Each time she re-shaped her lips into a vowel that sounded increasingly surprised.

Outside, the house turned progressively whiter. The summer sun dissolved into golden, vaporish rays in the trees. The bruise—he never asked how she got it—spread across the sky.

Ravenswood

The Nun rides the streetcar named Asylum to the end of the Asylum Lake line. There's no lake there, never was, but at least the buckled acres of parking lot becalmed before the abandoned shopping mall reflect the gliding shadows of circling gulls.

"End of the line, Sister," announces the Conductor; his name tag reads *Martin*. Conductor Martin rises from his seat in order to crank another name, the return destination, onto the front of the streetcar.

"I'm not in the habit of doing this," the Nun says from behind him. The Conductor hears the clack of the rosary beads girdled about her waist, and a rustle crackling with static electricity as she discards her woolly black robes, and as he turns still holding the crank, she knocks him silly with a blow from her missal.

When he regains consciousness the Conductor finds himself hanging from a hand strap toward the rear of the streetcar. The rosary binds his wrists. He's dressed—draped would be more accurate—in the Nun's black robes; her sensible shoes, untied, pinch his feet. At least she has pinned the *Martin* name tag from what was his conductor's uniform onto what is now his habit.

At the front of the streetcar, cranking a new destination, the Nun wears his uniform and conductor's hat. The blue jacket is too long for her arms; her breasts strain against the brass buttons. A shock of red hair tilts the hat at a rakish angle.

"When I was a child, I thought nuns must be bald," Martin recalls, and speaks the thought aloud in hopes of making conversation. "How wrong I was," he adds in what he hopes is an ingratiating tone.

She looks so jaunty as she thumbs tokens from his coin changer in the sunlight streaming through the front windows that he can't be angry with her. Gulls caw and yipe excitedly as if out on Asylum Lake the smelt are rising. Sparrows gang on a single tree and make it twitter. He suddenly realizes that yes, it's peaceful, even beautiful here at the end of the line to be a conductor stacking tokens in the sunlight. She reminds him so much of himself that he wants to emulate her. From his new perspective of dangling like a sausage, a rush of the pathetic emotion that a victim sometimes feels toward an oppressor overwhelms him: the illusion that such brutal attention is misguided love. He finds it poignantly flattering that this strange, undoubtedly fervent, religious woman has been driven to take such risks and employ such desperate measures to subdue him. What made her snap? he wonders. How often must she have sat unnoticed yearning for his attention? How many times at vespers did his name obliterate in her heart the name of the Lord?

"*Te amo, te amo*," he calls out to the Nun. It's as close as he can come to speaking Latin, a dead language that he hopes will sound sacred to her.

A miscalculation, for the Nun evidences little, if any, feeling for either dead languages or the Conductor—make that the ex-Conductor. Apparently, she has not confused him with the streetcar any more than a hijacker confuses the pilot with the airplane. Apparently, it is the streetcar itself she desires, that incredible conveyance with blue voltage sparking at the junctures of overhead cable, a vehicle part city, part dream.

Ding, ding. A blue spark crackles, electricity enough to depopulate Death Row jolts the rear wheels, and the streetcar embarks toward the destination she has chosen.

Swaying from the hand strap with his bound hands clasped as if in prayer, Sister Mary Martin can make out the lettering the Nun has cranked at the front of the streetcar, although, as it appears backward, he must decipher it letter by letter. D-O-O-W-S-N-E-V-A-R. Doowsnevar. R-A-V-E-N-S-W-O-O-D. That was never on his route! He's never heard of such a street or neighborhood before.

But then, he can't help wondering if he's experiencing partial amnesia from that concussion with the missal. The blocks the streetcar rattles down look only vaguely familiar, but perhaps that's because he's been displaced from his customary perspective gazing down rails of narrow-gauge track from the front of the car. Careening from the hand strap as the streetcar races between corner stops, he thinks the ride seems more herky-jerky than he remembers.

"Move to the rear!" the Nun yells over the hiss of pneumatic doors opening and slamming shut on the surprised faces of commuters who have not been given the chance to board.

In the rear, the ex-Conductor twirls from the hand strap, abstractly fingering his beads, feeling disoriented, forgotten, suffering like a martyr on the verge of a mystical experience.

"*Je t'aime, je t'aime*," he whines.

No answer. Clearly, the Nun couldn't care less about Romance languages. Through the rear window, among the crowd of commuters that wildly pursue the streetcar, futilely grasping for the grillwork on the rear platform, he can see vaguely familiar faces. Isn't that flushed gentleman furiously waving a transfer in his fist as if bidding farewell Mr. Hedmund, his old English teacher who used to warn him, "Martin, you're a dreamer and when dreamers wake, sometimes they find themselves digging ditches or punching transfers on streetcars"?

And that gimpy black man trying to hook the grille of the streetcar with his cane, isn't that Coach Bender, complete with his old football knee, who used to warn him, "If you don't open your eyes and smell the coffee, Marty-boy, you're going to blindside yourself." And that heavyset bleached blonde who's just tripped over her purse and is now being trampled by the others running down the curving streetcar track—take away twenty years and forty pounds and she might have been the woman who used to sign her letters to him *the Girl of Your Dreams*, a name she later shortened to *GOYD*.

He can't recall GOYD's real name anymore, but the mere thought of her now in the context of his current situation leaves him no choice but to reevaluate his relationship with the Nun. Tears, unsuccessfully searching for tracks on his face, roll helter-skelter down his cheeks as he realizes that now, when he has finally discovered that love is surrender, he's been wasting his time trying to surrender to the wrong person. It's not the Nun herself but her example that he should identify with. She's obviously a woman with the courage of her convictions, unafraid of commitment no matter the sacrifice it entails, someone willing to discipline her life around a vow. Had he committed himself to the streetcar when he was its conductor, perhaps it would have remained faithful to him and never seduced the Nun. His sins all become achingly clear—his insensitivity, his blindness (those letters the Girl of Your Dreams would write to him came, after a while, to be addressed to *Dear Mr. Oblivious*—later abbreviated to *Dear Mr. O*, as if she were writing love letters to a cipher), and the worst sin of all, lack of passion: he'd taken being a conductor for granted, treated it as merely a job, an identity he stripped off with the uniform, when, dear God!, it was his life.

Dear Mr. O strikes his head despairingly against the chrome handrail. Advertisements to which he's long been oblivious swim before his eyes. So these are the daydreams of silkier hair and ageless complexions upon which the hordes filing past him each day dwelled as they embarked on their journey together. He remembers all those days, weeks, years that he and the streetcar, now improbably named Ravenswood, have shared, intimately connected no matter how much traffic or how large the crowd. While commuters sat gabbing, or lost in newspapers, or gazing blankly out the window, Martin had registered, just below the threshold of consciousness, each nick in the track, hitch in the cable, surge of current, subtle whir, and shifting of gears. Oh, for those luminous hours between morning and evening rush, merrily clanging along on schedule down sunny streets.

He becomes bitter, glares at the Nun bouncing and chuckling on *his* air cushion seat, and wishes he could beat her knuckles bloody with a ruler, could make her stand in a corner with aching arms outstretched balancing a Bible on each palm, could deprive her of recess and banish her to the wardrobe closet.

But the Nun, now no longer a nun but a conductor in her own right, seems oblivious to all but the streetcar. Throttle open, bell clanging, and a fine sweat gathered like a mustache along her upper lip, suddenly boisterous as a gondolier, she breaks into song, its melody a cross between "funiculi funicula" and a hymn, its lyrics a psalm.

> *Although the Lord be high above*
> *He doth recall the lowly*
> *And deep within the secret heart*
> *The Lord shall surely know thee*

Her flashing teeth bite into the apple from the Conductor's lunch bag. Each crunch of the apple seems transmitted to the streetcar as if spikes of electricity were driving it forward in a more and more abandoned way, and Martin remembers drives down a country two-lane in his old Camaro with the Girl of His Dreams beside him, unzipping his trousers, urging him, *Faster, faster*, as if the way she touched him were actually propelling the car. If a motorcycle cop had been pursuing them then the way cops are pursuing the streetcar now, it would have looked to him as if the female passenger suddenly vanished, and though Martin was gripping the wheel and it was his foot on the gas, the Camaro was responding to what her tongue was doing.

> *I'll love Thee with mine own true heart*
> * Before the world I'll praise Thee*
> *Your love was there before the start*
> * Thy mercy doth amaze me*

With an enormous jolt, haloed in blue lightning, the streetcar leaps the track, and as it hurtles airborne Martin glances out the back window to see if he might catch one last glimpse of that woman who'd reminded him of GOYD. Instead, he sees the motorcycle cops pitching headfirst over their handlebars and the crowd pulling up in a way that's almost ceremonious, like a procession of mourners who have allowed the hearse to escape, as the streetcar plunges through a canopy of trees.

Ex-Conductor Martin, who was once so aware of any imperfection in the smooth steel rails, now feels the streetcar grinding savagely over earth, kicking up dust, crashing through bush. He feels his connection with the machine of whose identity he was once a part, slipping away, its familiar track a fading memory. He thinks of all the streets they've been down together, streets with their misleading, disappointing names: Blue Island—just an asphalt aisle through bankrupt factories; Sunset—a street perennially in the shadow of tenements; Tree Haven—an artery of concrete paved in broken glass. Why don't those streets bear the names that tell their stories? Grand View with its pawnshops, bars, and crack houses should be called Dead End. When was the last time the stains on tree-less Mulberry actually came from ripened berries? Better to call it Blood Street. And that noble-sounding intersection of Lincoln and State deserves to be Hooker and John. But Ravens-wood is Ravenswood.

The doors whoosh open long enough for the commut-ers of the woods to file on. Their somber dress makes Martin grateful for the first time that he is wearing the black robes of the Nun. The shadows of their cloaks darken shafts of sun. The Nun who has become the Conductor continues her hymn:

> *How precious are Thy thoughts to me*
> *How great Thy loving kindness*
> *How blind the man who cannot see*
> *That God will ease his blindness*

But the commuters of Doowsnevar can only croak in a split tongue that must be older than any dead language.

A blur of vegetation streams by, limbs whapping the win-dows; humidity beads into sweat on Martin's shaved head and streams down his wimple. He joins with his fellow commuters in croaking a hymn he didn't know he knew, like when he was a child and prayed in Latin, never really understanding the words or what it was for which he prayed.

Brisket

Their pale, plump skins scorched almost to bursting, the Thuringers invited a plaster of brown mustard.

The stacked pastrami was decked out in zooty 1950s colors: blushing pink meat in a carapace of black pepper.

There was corned beef awaiting horseradish, kosher franks and kraut, dangling salamis, *tukus*, house hickory-smoked turkey, trout, sablefish, and two kinds of knishes—thin kasha and golden squares of potato—slaw, paprika-dusted potato salad, fried onions and schmaltz, green tomatoes, kaiser rolls, baguettes, pumpernickel. I'd been walking around all day in the cold and it all looked good. But finally, when my turn in line arrived, I decided to invest my last few dollars in the garlic-kissed brisket on rye.

"Young man, I'm going to make you a very nice sandwich," murmured the old, bald server, wearing a stained white apron.

He said it conspiratorially, his lips barely moving, drawing me toward him in order to hear, as if it were something he'd rather the owners of the establishment not get wind of. A secret between the two of us, not for the ears of the others behind me in line.

He glanced up into my eyes and held them as if he'd taken a personal interest in me, which was more than I could say for the secretaries and interviewers in the personnel offices where

I'd spent the last six weeks filling out applications for jobs while my money ran out and I moved from friend to friend, crashing from apartment to apartment, sleeping on sofas and floors as if I'd never grow up if I stayed poor. His face, cross-hatched in lines, was set in the comically tragic expression he'd practiced until it had become his permanent physiognomy. He must have been making sandwiches for a long time, must have seen a lot of hungry faces staring back at him from the other side of the glass partition.

Maybe he'd learned to read faces at a glance and could read in mine that a desperation I'd never felt before was setting in. That I needed a helping hand. That I'd caught enough of a glimpse of what it meant to be down, homeless, jobless, walking the streets hungry to last a lifetime.

Or maybe to get through the day he allowed himself now and then to take a liking to the face of a perfect stranger. A face that perhaps reminded him of himself when he was young, or of someone in his past, the way that, riding the subway and watching all the people with jobs filing on, I'd sometimes see a woman who would remind me of an old girlfriend in another city, a city I should have stayed in, a girlfriend I should have stayed with. That same girlfriend who once told me, "You've got a working-class face."

Maybe he thought so, too.

"See?" he said, surgically trimming off the fat with the tip of his carving knife, and then scraping the trimmings across the cutting-board counter, leaving a trail of grease. That's when I noticed the numbers tattooed on his wrist. I'd seen the faded marks of the death camps on the wrists of tailors in that neighborhood before. Those tattooed numbers still shocked me into a sense of dislocation. The brutal reality of history crowded out the mundane present. I wondered what he thought when he looked at his wrist every day. What horrible memories did he overcome each morning? When I saw those numbers I felt ashamed. Here I was spending my last few bucks—big deal! I would survive.

"How about some nice scraps for your dog?" he asked, gesturing with his knife to the pile of trimmings that he'd been accumulating from mine and other sandwiches. Attached to the fat were hearty-looking ribbons of brisket. There was at least another meal there.

"Sure," I said.

"Okay," he said, still with that confidential tone as if something preferential were going on between us.

Working in a practiced methodical sequence, he wrapped the trimmings in waxed paper and the waxed paper in a sheet of brown butcher paper which he expertly folded into a neat, tight, easily concealed packet before taping it and handing it toward me. "Only two dollars."

"Two dollars?"

"For your dog," he said.

I thought he'd been offering to give them away and suddenly I felt like a total fool. All at once it struck me that whatever had made me naïve enough to think the scraps might be free was the same impulse that had landed me in my current situation: out of work, living from friend to friend, missing a woman in another city, a woman who'd already given up on me.

"I don't have a dog," I told him.

"You just said you had one."

"I used to have one."

"You forgot you don't have a dog anymore?" He couldn't get over that someone could make such a mistake.

"I had a dog but he died. I still say yes out of force of habit."

"I'm sorry to hear about your dog."

"Thanks," I said. "He was a schnauzer named Yappy. Happy

Yappy I used to call him. He sure would have liked those scraps."

"Maybe you have a cat?"

"No cat," I said.

"You sure now?"

"Positive."

"Want a garlicky pickle with that?"

"How much?" I asked. I'd learned my lesson.

"Comes with the sandwich."

Alms

After Mr. Kronner's daily constitutional down Eighty-sixth to the river and back, Mattie wheeled him under the scaffolding and into the lobby. Workmen had been refurbishing the building for months and the dark scaffolding had come to seem a permanent feature. At least they'd installed an automatic door and a ramp so that Mattie no longer needed help pushing the chair through the entrance and up the short flight of stairs to the elevator. Valentine, the doorman, still would usually push the chair along with her as if the incline required his added muscle. She and Valentine had a running conversation going in which Valentine would tell her new places in Astoria where he'd find fruits and fish from the islands.

"Hey, Chicken Legs, guess what I find at the market?" he'd ask. "Old wife! Fresh on ice, not smelling, not frozen. Never thought I'd see old wife in this city, me son."

Valentine was from St. Croix. Back home she'd heard that the Crucians thought they were better than Tortolans. "Just because they on Uncle Sammy's dole," her mother used to say. But here in New York, it was as if she and Valentine had been childhood friends. Mattie didn't mind that he called her Chicken Legs; she knew that it was his way of giving a compliment.

Today, Valentine merely waved from where he stood at the curb tugging at the leashes of three shivering whippets while hailing a cab for Mrs. Takamura so that she could take her dogs for a run in Central Park.

At the service elevator, which Mattie always used when she was pushing the chair, one of the men working on the building held the elevator door while Mattie wheeled in Mr. Kronner.

"Excuse us, sorry, thank you," Mattie said as she accidentally rolled the chair over the man's foot.

The man nodded, as if apologizing for not speaking because his mouth was full—he was chewing a sandwich. He squeezed on behind Mattie and the door closed.

He was wearing a Glidden's paper painter's cap and jeans that looked clean even though there were spots from faded white paint or maybe from bleach along the thighs. In the loop below his right pocket, a claw hammer hung. Otherwise, he was nondescript, one of those mutt-like guys with a stubbly beard and an acne-pitted face who could have been Hispanic or black or Mideastern or even white. It wasn't how he looked that was important so much as how he didn't look— not one of the homeless that you couldn't walk down Eighty-sixth without being accosted by, begging for a handout or trying to sell you *StreetWise*, or some paperback book or magazine they'd fished out of the trash and spread out in a sidewalk display. Did anyone ever buy any of those books? There was a homeless man who stood at the intersection on Third with a spray bottle and a rag and would wash windshields, and a little man called Pygmy with a bag and a whisk broom wired to a stick who followed people walking their dogs and offered, for a dollar, to clean up after them. Yesterday, over by the park along the river, a homeless man had come up to her, holding in his hand a green parakeet that must have escaped somebody's house, and tried to sell it. The bird looked so luminescent and delicate in the man's dirty fist that Mattie would have liked it, if only to release it again, but Mr. Kronner made it clear that they were to give nothing to people he considered bums. The man on the elevator wasn't a bum and he wasn't some gangster like the kid with dreadlocks she'd just seen on Eighty-sixth, prying in broad daylight with a piece of pipe at the lock on a delivery bike chained to a stop sign and cursing passersby aloud as if it were their fault he couldn't snap the chain. Instead of work boots, the man on the elevator wore tennis shoes—but they weren't high-tops. And he was eating, like a workingman too busy to break for lunch, tearing at a croissant sandwich wrapped in foil so that his dirty hand wouldn't soil his food. That simple act of gobbling lunch on the fly made him seem unthreatening, and he'd held the door open so politely, too. He smiled at her.

"Thank you," Mattie said again. She was always saying thank you around Mr. Kronner, as if trying to make up for the fierce, angry way he stared at everyone, not that he could help it. His face was stuck in that expression. If Mr. Kronner had not been there she might have said what she was thinking, which was to warn the man to be careful not to accidentally bite off a piece of foil that would then touch one of his fillings.

"No problem," the man said between chews.

Mr. Kronner stabbed the 25 button with his cane, as was his habit. It was the only time he used the cane. Certainly he couldn't walk or even use it to help him stand. He was like a child about wanting to press the elevator buttons. The doors closed and the car ascended.

"What floor you want?" Mattie asked. "He'll press it for you."

"Twenty-six," the man mumbled, his mouth stuffed.

"Only goes to twenty-five," Mattie said.

He'd balled up the foil and stuffed what was left of the sandwich into his mouth and put his hand out as if to say, Sorry, can't talk just now.

They rode in silence to twenty-five and when they reached it, the man stepped out to hold the door open again, barring her way at the same time. He took out his hammer and braced it between the elevator door and the doorjamb.

"I got a knife," he said to Mattie. "You need to see it?"

"What?" she asked.

"You heard me. You need to see it or do you believe me that this is happening?"

"I believe you," she said quietly.

"You should. This is the Big Apple, babe."

"What you want? He's old," Mattie said, looking down at Mr. Kronner. His eyes were wild-looking, the left one bulged and roved about seemingly with a will of its own that made it appear even more furious-looking than his right eye, which was watering. Above his eyes, his eyebrows perched like gray wings of some bird of prey. He refused to let Mattie or anyone trim those eyebrows. His hawk nose was like a peeling beak. He leaned forward on his cane.

"What's his problem?" the man asked.

"Had a stroke."

"He shouldn't be looking like that at me. Crabby old motherfuck."

"He don't mean nothing."

"Empty the purse, gimme the old man's wallet. Gimme the watch."

"No wallet," Mattie said. "I carry the money in my purse."

"Where you get that accent, girl?" the man said, falling into a mocking accent.

"Tortola," she said.

"What you do for this nasty old piece of white cheese, Tortola, besides wheel him around like a baby?"

Mattie said nothing.

"You play with his old pud?"

She said nothing.

"A fucking Timex! And there's only twenty fucking dollars in here," he said, throwing down the purse.

"That's all we ever carry."

"Who's in his apartment besides you two?"

"His son, Val," Mattie lied. "Home from college."

"Pull your dress up."

"Please," she said.

"Don't argue with a knife, stupid Tortola." He slipped a thick black-handled jackknife out of his pocket and opened it up. The blade looked tarnished and dull, dirty like the hand that held it. "See, you didn't believe me."

"I believed you."

"Nice skinny legs. Shaving them, I see. They don't shave their legs down in Tortola, do they? You come here to New York and get trendy, girl?"

Mattie was crying, silently. She glanced at Mr. Kronner, who sat with his usual impassively fierce expression but his left eye roving and gleaming as if out of control.

"Pull down the panties. Maybe you be shaving your pussy, too."

She stared at him.

"Listen, Tortola, I'm taking a chance taking extra time to fuck with you, so don't mess around or I'm gonna have to be mean. What I tell you to do you fucking do, crybaby. It's Mr. Crabby Cheapass's lucky day. He's gonna get a little show for his money."

Two weeks later, when Mattie was wheeling Mr. Kronner across Eighty-sixth Street at Second Avenue, the old man suddenly stuck his cane into the spokes of a delivery bike and sent the Asian kid riding it flying headlong over the handlebars into the back of a cab. The kid lay dazed on the street, his arms flailing in a mess of crushed white cartons spilling soup, noodles, and sauce. He was trying to get up, swearing or pleading for help in a language Mattie didn't understand a word of, while the cabbie, a Hindu in a turban, stood by his open door on the driver's side waving traffic by and shouting after his passenger, who was fleeing the cab through the other door, apparently without paying his fare.

"Not my fault, not my fault!" the cabbie repeated.

A homeless man who'd been waiting by the light, the only person besides her, as far as Mattie could see, who'd witnessed what Mr. Kronner had done, stared at Mr. Kronner, who sat in his chair looking impassively fierce, but his left eye roving and gleaming in a way that Mattie had seen only once before— on the elevator that day they'd been assaulted. She thought the roving of his eye had been a symptom of panic then, but now it somehow suggested a crazed mirth. The homeless man had retrieved Mr. Kronner's cane from the street, handed it back to him, and was now staring Mattie in the eyes. She recognized him from among the other homeless men she passed each day. He was the man who had tried to sell her the parakeet he'd caught. He nodded hello, then stretched out his hand, and Mattie opened her purse and gently laid a crisp twenty-dollar bill onto his dirty, trembling palm.

Here Comes the Sun

A strawberry blonde slams out of the conch-shell-pink Paradise taxi and, strappy white heels dangling from one hand and a sisal purse from the other, walks barefoot across the hot sand, her eyes fixed on the sea.

Not so much as a glance at the goats munching sea grapes, at the guinea fowl shrieking among shorebirds, at Itchy Mon, the brindled mongrel sniffing after her perfume, which is perhaps what prompts him to lift a leg against an ylang-ylang tree. Not a glance even at the mounds of faded pink conch shells that mark the graves of the fishermen buried where they once fished shark from the beach—Shark Beach—and don't be telling the tourists it's called that, me son—night fishing that by the blaze of driftwood bonfires looked like a tug-of-war with the ocean. Anchor chain for leader, a rotted goat head for bait, Rest in Peace.

The living attract no more notice from her than the dead. She passes the Coco Mon, his machete whittling green coconuts down to their water; and a Charles Atlas with skin the color of squid ink, who's walking on his hands; and Itchy Mon's master, whose face beneath a disheveled straw hat is shadow and a smile as he clonks from a steel drum the only song he seems to know; and the dancer with a gray, dreadlocked beard, Neptune wearing a hula skirt of dying octopus and conducting with a trident spear.

Near the water's sloshing edge she stakes out a towel-sized patch of sand—not that she has a towel—drops her bag and high heels, then kneels, unbuttons her white cotton blouse, and slips it off.

Her lacy white bra exposes less than a bikini top. Still, Basinio Davis, tall for his age, a junior high kid who wants to go to the States and play for the Chicago Bulls, has witnessed a legend: I was there, me son, the day this *blanc* lady comes to the Shark and takes off her clothes.

There's a constellation of freckles under her bra straps. She squirms out of her black skirt. Her white panties reflect the sunlight. She folds the blouse on top of the skirt, weights them with her flimsy shoes, and, sisal bag for a pillow, stretches out on the bare hot sand. Me son, only the little kids run around this beach in their undies. Once some French showed up and went topless, but that's different.

It's how she's stripped off her clothes. Not like some exhibitionist, but like a woman who no longer feels there's time to be conventional. Despite the streets in town lined with free-port shops, there apparently wasn't time enough to buy a swimsuit or a souvenir towel or even a tube of lotion to keep her pale skin from burning. Maybe she came to this island for a quickie divorce and has a plane to catch back to someplace buried in snow. Maybe she's dumping some cheat she once worshipped in the way she just knelt before the sea. Or maybe a man who loved her too much is letting her go, maybe it has become unbearable for him when business associates learn how casually her clothes are discarded.

If it were you, would you hail a pink Paradise taxi and find your way to where you could be a total stranger for an afternoon, on a nameless beach on the native side of the island? Would the sound in your mind be the scream of a guinea fowl, the lap of the sea, or the lilting notes from an old man playing a perpetual-motion "Here Comes the Sun" on the pans?

Her eyes are closed. No one asks, What is it you hear? She wouldn't answer anyway.

But oblivious though she's seemed, she must feel the stares because she raises her head suddenly as if determined to confront the gaze of whatever creep can't summon the courtesy to give a woman alone on a beach she'll never have the chance to see again a moment's peace, and her eyes meet the eyestalks of a dozen ghost crabs waltzing sideways around her body.

And I say it's all right.

Coat

A coat from another life comes up behind him and like an old flame slips its limp arms around his shoulders. He watches as they dance in the mirror—he and his coat. He slides his arms into its sleeves. His hands fill up its pockets.

Look at the street, that avenue of wind we used to flare, my coat and I. He knows that one can't step into the same street twice, and yet he's returned to this city looking not for the eternal, but for whatever has survived.

Nothing has changed, the coat believes. It's said a coat can make the man, but the coat knows that the man shapes it as wind does a sail. It's a man who brings a coat to life, then shrugs it off and leaves it waiting.

All the time spent hanging in the dark on the hunched shoulders of the wooden hanger from the Hotel Luna seems to the coat merely an extended change of season, a predictable cycle in which nothing more significant than weather has happened. Take a coat off; put a coat on. What occurs in between isn't the coat's concern.

The coat may be right, the man thinks. He recalls the impulse to go away and leave the coat behind, but not what, if anything, he was hoping to find. Now it seems almost as though it were someone other than himself who was off strolling in shirtsleeves and sunglasses through a palpable brightness—a figure in rolled-up duck pants disappearing down a dazzling road that unaccountably ended in a maze of goat trails twisting into mangroves where the only other pedestrians were mobs of crabs brandishing their claws like machetes. Perhaps whoever it was behind those mirrored sunglasses is still throwing a shadow where the sea slops over rotten tennis shoes; perhaps whoever it was has made his way past smoldering coal pots and old men slapping down dominoes outside of rum shops, to one of a run of hotel rooms that seemed to rotate beneath the crank of a ceiling fan, rooms smelling of empty bottles, with scorpions in the shower and closets that were never meant for an overcoat, rooms in which each morning he sorted through a mildewed suitcase of strewn laundry for a shirt without discolored underarms.

And all the while he was gone, the coat hung suspended and believed that the man, too, hung somewhere, in storage, asleep on a hanger of bone, dreaming as the coat dreamed, of snowy light shafting through dusty windows into a drafty warehouse of disrobed mannequins.

Put a coat on, and it's resurrected, standing tall in a full-length mirror, a timelessly fashionable knee-length gray-green herringbone reappraising itself at the threshold of a familiar reflection.

What if stepping back into a life could be as simple as slipping on an old coat? Suppose, as if in some tale, the coat might serve as a magic raiment that a man beloved by a goddess puts on to receive a gift of power, the way an ancient hero might attire himself in invincible armor, a cloak of invisibility, winged sandals.

It's not invisibility or armor that the man needs, but a coat of attachment, a garment that when buttoned back on might reconnect him to the time when he was still recognizably himself before he stepped over the border of who he'd meant to be. He turns from his reflection, which also turns, retreating into the mirror and refusing to follow him out. The coat doesn't retreat, and the man allows it to guide him as they step onto the street.

It was a labyrinthine route we used to take, the coat recalls, a journey via fabulous conveyances that instead of detachment should have caused a daily astonishment: down the vanishing steps of escalators, through turnstiles that one cranked with the hip thrust of a lover—long lines of commuters bundled in coats, thrusting, each morning, through ringing turnstiles. A dash along underground corridors, past blue switches still burning from night. Doors slam. The train shoots through the tunnel like a memorandum through a pneumatic tube.

The man in the coat emerges, a part of the crowd with its collective consciousness of fragmented headlines and daydreams, filing into a glass door revolving like a device that sorts crowds back into individuals. He ascends in an elevator that climbs a glass column as silently as a fever reading in a thermometer. Chrome doors slide open onto a floor of office space where walls of windows eye-level with the undersides of smoldering clouds overlook the gray projections of downtown. Beside each desk, a coat draped with the banner of a scarf waits on a hook shared with an umbrella. The man, still wearing his coat, sits at a desk, flicks on the computer, recalls his password *DeusAderit*, which he lifted from the inscription on Carl Jung's tombstone: *Vocatus atque non vocatus Deus aderit. Called or uncalled, God is present.* He types, *Welcome back,* but the words refuse to appear on the screen.

Evening: luminescent empty offices stacked against the sky; the cry of a street musician's trumpet counterpoints the percussion of rush-hour L trains. A misty drizzle dissipates the odor of mothballs and the coat releases its true scent, not smoke or the perfume absorbed in restaurants or bars, but woolliness that the man imagines to be the smell of sheep musky with salt fog on some craggy island in the North Sea.

The man doesn't mind when the coat hurries them past Goodwill and used-clothing shops. He doesn't mind stopping when the coat, vain as always, pauses to regard its reflection in the black plate-glass window of the Twenty-first, a bar where they would go regularly after work for an Irish whiskey. Just a quick one to burn off the aftertaste of a workday, though more often than not he'd end up throwing dice for drinks with a boisterous bunch from the "Subs"—the Foreign Subsidiaries Department.

"Max, old boy, take off your coat and stay awhile," they'd urge.

When the Subs said they regarded themselves as a cosmopolitan crowd it meant that that was an evening when they were drinking cosmopolitans. There were cosmopolitan evenings, Manhattan evenings, Black Russian evenings, mojito evenings, highball evenings, absinthe evenings . . .

"Max, my friend," one of them—Willis—might ask, "have you ever endured a time when something in your life felt as corrosive as the rim of salt on a margarita?"

And another—Ricardo—would add, "Ah, Max, our dead-language scholar, always the loner, did I ever tell you, my friend, how I once had a girlfriend named Carmelita who made me feel like the *libre* in a Cuba libre. Have you ever loved a woman like that, Max? Skin the shade her name suggests, and when she was aroused, a smell to her body of scorched sugar and fermented cane."

"*Salute!*" the Subs would chant in chorus, raising their Cuba libres to Ricardo.

With the coat flopped over an empty barstool beside him—as it is now—Max would drink a simple double whiskey, or two, or three. And when finally back outside—as he and his coat are now—he'd feel flushed with the addicting mix of excitement and anesthesia that drinking in the early evening never failed to bring on. He feels that flush again. *Welcome back*, the words that refused to form on the computer screen, glow on the window of the bar. The reflection makes it appear as if the coat is alone, with no one wearing it, as if it stands levitating, ghostly beneath a dripping awning.

Evening surges in gusts. While he was inside the bar the drizzle became a drumming rain. Rain falls in four dimensions. Whether the window of the Twenty-first reflects the present or the past is uncertain. In the present, memory smells like rain and there's time to inhale breath after breath. But in the past, where remembering is inconceivable, Max needs to catch a cab or he'll be late for a first date with a woman he's met earlier that day in the employees' cafeteria. She was sitting by herself sipping a coffee and reading a paperback. He sat down at the next table and asked, "Good book?"

"Not bad." She smiled. "Dante."

"Shhh," he cautioned, "you don't want to say things like that too loud around here. It's bad enough that you're making a spectacle of yourself reading in public."

"It's for a night class I'm taking," she said.

"No excuse," he told her. "A class in what?"

"'A History of Visions.'"

"You must be new. I haven't seen you before."

She'd been hired a week earlier, she said, as a receptionist in Foreign Subs. Stationing her at the desk out front must be giving Subs a continental flair, he thought. With her dark glossy hair and olive eyes, she looked as if she might speak with a foreign accent. Her All-American name, Betty, didn't seem to fit.

Later, she'll tell him how even as a child her name felt like an alias. Once, she asked her mother, "Why'd you name me Betty?" and her mother answered, "Dear me, I don't recall." She'll tell him that as a child she felt that her mother might be an imposter, too.

Betty agrees to meet for a drink after work, just not at the bar where the Subs hang out. She chooses the Surfside, a singles bar he knows by reputation, the kind of place he ordinarily avoids. The Surfside is at least a mile from water. It would take a tsunami to hear the crash of surf.

"Promise you won't be late," Betty tells him. "I get nervous sitting in bars alone. Guys don't leave you in peace."

"I don't suppose they do," he says.

Later, Betty will ask if he's seeing anyone. He'll say no; she'll say, me neither. Really? he'll ask. She'll say there'd been a discreet fling with a Corvette dealer who played bass in an oldies rock band and was seeing Noreen, a girlfriend of hers who's a hospice nurse, so it was complicated. Complicated is a word Betty uses whenever she mentions the 'Vette dealer. It means they kept things secret and just when the sex got really hot between them—"our amazing connection, a magical mystery tour," the 'Vette guy called it—he dumped her without an explanation, at least not one that she believed. She hasn't been serious about anyone since.

He keeps checking his watch and tries hailing a cab. Traffic is snarled to a standstill. He could walk faster than he could ride, but then he'd show up looking foolish—liquor on his breath, hair plastered down, his glasses in need of windshield wipers. He'd hoped to make an urbane impression. Instead of having arrived early enough to order a drink for himself and to fold his coat over a barstool so as to save her a seat, and then to sit nervously waiting for her to show, he will be the one who's late, and the rain is falling harder.

Later, his first time in her bedroom with its bare white walls, lying beside her in bed, she coaxes him into reciting the profound thoughts he wrote down as poems in high school, something about "Time receding, erasing the past . . ." And she asks, I wonder what would have happened had we met as kids? Would we have felt the same connection? Probably, he says, but we might have had to delay the sleepover. She laughs and says, I'm trying to reorient myself, I mean, I can still count backward to when we first kissed—only thirteen days ago! You're an amazing kisser, he says. That's what you told me that night, she says, and the next day I called to say you were my first thought in the morning, and you called us a work in progress. And now look, we're supposed to be watching the State of the Union Address and instead we're in a state of half-undressed with no idea where this country is headed. That could be serious. Serious is fine, he says, just so long as it isn't complicated. And she says, Thanks for complicating things even more.

He's never noticed before how rain simultaneously rains at different speeds: one for the drops beating off the pavement, spattering his shoes and cuffs; another, faster, for rain streaking through the beams of headlights and the streetlights that have just blinked on; and a third speed for the rain chuting from the scalloped edge of the awning.

Still later, in a conversation he will never forget, in winter, she'll say, It's too cold to be walking with your coat open. They're walking from a bar to the train station, both tipsy. Betty is leaving for a long weekend to visit her friend Noreen and he's carrying her suitcase—carrying it rather than rolling it because of the dirty slush. He tells her that it's more trouble than it's worth to stop to button his coat. He'd have to put the suitcase down in the slush and take off his gloves. And she replies, I'd kneel in the cold street to button your coat.

The coat on the black window of the bar raises its collar. Just on the other side of the window the tipsy bunch from Subs are rolling dice and saying, "I feel like the bitters in an Orange Blossom."

"I feel like the grub at the bottom of a bottle of mescal."

"I feel as blue as blue Curaçao."

Later, she'll ask, Remember that first time you joked about undressing down to our concealed weapons? I do, he says.

I'm sorry it wasn't funny—I was so nervous. I'm all in, she
says, there's no more need of protection between us. I want
you to have all the pleasure a woman can give.

Blocks away the new receptionist, Betty—a name whose
whispered, soft explosive *B* his lips have yet to learn—Betty,
who tonight wears her hair pinned up ballet-style and looks
as if she's come from a town named Cortina or Palermo but
probably hails from somewhere like Peoria or Decatur, is wearing a pink raincoat and red heels. Despite the grass stains that
couldn't be dry-cleaned out, her raincoat, sworn to be discreet,
won't reveal how, at a drunken party, a salt-and-pepper-bearded
man in a red-and-black leather Corvette jacket stripped off
the raincoat and threw it down beneath their bodies on the
wet grass. Betty sits with her legs crossed in a soon-to-be-
razed bar called the Surfside. It will be the wrecking ball, not
a tsunami, that demolishes it, but at this moment Betty isn't
worried about its fate. She's impatiently wondering if Max—
she doesn't even know his last name yet—will show and why
he's late after she made him promise to be on time, and although she's annoyed, when he finally arrives, apologetic,
dripping, his hair plastered, his glasses spattered, and tells
her, "You're like the Galliano in a Harvey Wallbanger," she
has to laugh. She removes his glasses and wipes them dry on
the hem of her raincoat, a gesture that exposes her thigh. No
matter what they're calling tonight at the Twenty-first, here at
the Surfside it's going to be a Harvey Wallbanger night.

Later, in early spring, after he sees the first convertible of
the year with its top dropped—a candy-apple-red 'Vette with
a pink raincoat riding shotgun beside a bearded driver in
oldies rock bandanna headwear and dark glasses—he'll ask
Betty, Is there something you should tell me? She'll act
offended and insist there's nothing and he'll say, I should tell
you, to save us both the embarrassment, that I already know,
and Betty will say, Look at my face, look into my eyes, I swear

to you. He'll remember she's an alias with a mother who is an imposter. He'll spend a weekend watching her lie. He'll finally ask, If you don't love me enough to tell me the truth, at least tell me, do I need to go get tested? And Betty will answer: The truth inhibits me.

The neon lights, despite their false starts, have flickered on. In the sprayed headlights of stalled traffic, the wet street looks sleek and shiny. He plunges out from under the awning into the procession of bobbing umbrellas, and zigzags through the downpour like a broken-field runner, dodging past those who aren't late tonight for whatever destiny awaits them.

Later, just before he puts a few things worth saving— books, photographs, a coat—in storage and buys a ticket out of his life, he'll translate her phrase, "The truth inhibits me," into Latin. Probitas me cohibet. *A classic phrase like that deserves the gravitas of a dead language, he thinks. It could be cast as a motto on a medallion or a family crest or an epitaph on a gravestone. Maybe there'd be a market for it on a T-shirt. Then he remembers Willis's question: Have you ever endured a time when something in your life felt as corrosive as the rim of salt on a margarita?*

He'd be better off running in the opposite direction through the three speeds of rain away from the bar, but he's outdistanced whatever advice or hunches the past or the future might afford him. He's back in pace with the present as if he's never left it, as if he'll never leave it again.

The coat can barely keep up.

He breaks free of the crowd, tightropes along the curb avoiding parking meters, hits full stride, gathering momentum to hurdle the flooded gutter, and then launches from the corner of Rush and Walton—a man leaping higher than necessary to clear a puddle, some guy in midair with his coat flying.

Fedora

Remove it and there's sunlight. Terraced vineyards, a grove of olive trees, the netting of an old bridal gown shading the staked tomato plants, the sound of a distant accordion squeezed in time to the swish of the sea.

Remove it and it's as if you've lifted off the weight of memory. Memory that was once so companionable, and that now has turned into an assassin. Memory with its offended honor, with its vendetta, giving you the evil eye like the godmother of a jilted bride. You work the razor along your throat while, veiled in dust, the bride stares back from a mirror framed in black like a sympathy card, an antique mirror whose fly spots have become freckles of age, whose spidery cracks and broken capillaries have reassembled into the image of your face juxtaposed upon her face, a mirror whose motto is "*J'accuse.*"

Remove it and there's the tintinnabulation of shells as the sea laps the sand. Crystalline blue water spattered by flying fish. A lemon grove in blossom. And beyond the bees, the sound of a river. And across the river on a distant bank of sunflowers, someone cupping a harmonica.

But put it on and its brim of shadow extends until there's barely enough light to see the five steps leading down to the wet street. The moon the backside of a mirror; streetlamps in tulle. And from a black-framed doorway, exactly like the doorway you've stepped through, straightening his hat as you straighten yours, an assassin also descends five steps, pausing only to strike and cup a match. In the blue flare, you recognize the face as your face, the same face imprinted on all you've come to kill.

Goodwill

After considerable deliberation, the woman selects a jade slip from the rack of vintage lingerie. When she disappears into the dressing booth, Gil follows, and attempts to sneak behind the curtain after her.

"Excuse me! Excuse me, young man," Madame Proprietor calls, rising up behind her antique cash register and peering over her bifocal lorgnette. Madame has cultured a way of enunciating that expresses profound disapproval—an enunciation that makes shouting unnecessary and yet turns every head in the store. "The peep show is two blocks south on Clark."

Gil never sees Bea wearing the jade slip, but he and a triptych of mirrors do get to admire the poses she strikes in a violet feathered boa that Zelda might have Charlestoned wearing. "A must-have," Gil says, "though it seems to be molting." A Jackie O pink pillbox hat with what Madame calls a French-netted veil follows the boa. The netting is torn, and when Gil asks if that's a metaphor for Camelot, Madame answers, "Say what?"

Next, a pearly Jazz Age dress with a plunging neckline and what Madame refers to as a handkerchief hemline. Madame pairs the dress with a deco tiara for what Gil refers to as a priestess-of-Osiris vibe. There's an aubergine velvet beret, perfect for an aperitif with Sartre, which, Gil says, is worth the price, despite the spot that looks like pigeon droppings. There's a sleeveless sequined top whose shimmer transforms Bea into the Blue Angel. When Gil says so, she shows her legs and sings in a German accent, "*Falling in love again, never wanted to, what am I to do . . .*" She pauses. "I don't remember what's next."

"*Can't help it,*" Gil tells her.

"I can't," she says. "How about you?"

"Apparently not."

Clothes, Bea once told Gil, can be a kind of diary. She doesn't keep a journal like he does, but the clothes—going as far back as high school—that jam her closets, hang like chapters of a shape-changing life. Journals tell one kind of truth, and dresses, Bea says, tell another, different story. Bea doesn't go shopping; she goes "antiquing": she goes "junking." Goodwill might be a second-hand shop to some, but for Bea its racks hold fragmented histories waiting to be reanimated.

A leopard-dyed rabbit-fur jacket completes the ensemble of a tiger-striped satin skirt, alligator pumps, and a wampum necklace that Bea calls her mixed-species look. There's a crisp white shirt with a raised collar, and when Madame suggests that it's exactly the shirt that Katharine Hepburn wore with trousers, Gil asks if Hepburn sweated profusely. Despite the underarms, he admits it's got the look. "Just remember while wearing it," he says, "not to wave goodbye."

Finally, it's time to bargain with the Madame, who, when the subject is no longer sex but money, raises her voice as if it is the customer who were hard of hearing. Gil has never been good at bargaining, and watches impressed as Bea and Madame go head to head. For a few bucks, Bea purchases an ivory crepe de chine scarf. It would appear she is buying vapor if not for the scarf's faint threading of wine-colored stripes. As soon as they step outside, she uses it to throttle him.

In her bedroom, the vapor comes to life, slithering about Bea's throat and breasts like the serpent seducing Eve.

"I wish everything I wore could make me feel this light,"

she says, then whispers, "It feels like you're slipping it through my body," when he draws the scarf between her thighs. Gil blindfolds her with it and demands she guess what's coming next. The more she's proved correct, the more boldly explicit her guesses become.

Bea pairs the scarf with a simple black dress to wear to dinner. The restaurant is called Violet. The small pots of violets on each table are lights. Violet lighting blossoms from the bare brick walls. Its glow tints the mirrors and the blank white sheets of Japanese handmade paper and turns the scarf amethyst. The champagne racing in their flutes is tinted, too.

"Special occasion?" the waiter inquires.

"That obvious?" Gil asks, and the waiter smiles.

"I've noticed when you mislead waiters, your penance is always to overtip," Bea says, after the waiter is gone.

"Who misled anyone? It *is* a special occasion."

"What occasion is that?"

"We'll know once we look back on it," Gil says. "It's thanks to our cheap date at Goodwill, not to mention your frugality and hard bargaining, we can afford to celebrate."

The store where she bought the scarf was actually named Madame's, but Bea refers to any second-hand vintage clothing store as Goodwill.

"Poor you, getting dragged along junking," she says.

"It wasn't so bad. Sort of like entering a time machine. Who knows where we'll end up next time."

"I'm afraid I can't invite you again."

"I promise to behave better."

"Sorry, taking you to Goodwill is too dangerous."

"Goodwill dangerous? How?"

"Because despite your disregard for fashionistas, pretentious proprietors, and musty shops, and your barely concealed aversion to the stained, ratty discards of strangers, you'd have me buying everything."

Dark Ages

After midnight, when the only café insists on closing, they follow the corkscrew street that leads like every other street in the village to the Fountain of Nymphs. If they can find the fountain, then, even in this darkness, they can find their hotel, which overlooks the fountain, although their room does not. Through their shuttered window that opens outward into palm fronds, they can hear the fountain all night keeping time with its plashing. Or is it that rather than *keeping* time, the fountain makes time inconsequential—at least for as long as their money holds out? Each night the echoing cascade lulls them to sleep. By morning, the burble of water is barely audible above the hubbub of foreign voices already going about their business.

Of course it's their own voices that are foreign here where they have no business, where they've arrived by accident—another in a succession of accidents between them, but, so far, an accident in which no one's been seriously hurt. Even their laughter sounds foreign and out of place as they hike back from the café. She trails her fingers as if feeling her way along the rugged walls of the stone houses that line the unlit narrow street.

"Shhh," they shush each other, and laugh.

"We have to keep it down," he says. They stop and kiss hard as if to seal each other's lips, dizzily lose their balance, and steady themselves against a wall. With her back braced, he draws her hips toward him, and their bodies press together.

"You're not following your own advice," she says.

"What advice?"

"To keep it down," she whispers, and then bursts into tipsy laughter.

Above cratered cobblestones, the moon is a blank in a starless sky. When the café sign blinks out behind them, he tells her they must have entered the Dark Ages.

In the entire village, only a single streetlight above the fountain still burns. Its electricity seems an anachronism; it should be burning beeswax or whale oil or kerosene. Given the glare, they're probably lucky their room doesn't face the fountain. In the harsh yellow light, the fountain appears to be crumbling, fissured, eroded by its own gush of water. Each day, workmen patch the cracks and skim leaves and debris off the fountain pool with long-handled nets that look as if they'd be good for catching butterflies. But like a recurring troubled dream, after dark the cracks reappear and leaks spout and puddle the cobblestones so that it looks as if a rainstorm has just swept the square. Tiny tributaries, each with its own current, trace the sloping street down "the thousand steps." Step by step, water trickles toward the village on the hillside below. Instead of a Fountain of Nymphs, that village is famous for the corpse of its patron saint, which refuses to rot. Given the choice between a village with a Fountain of Nymphs and a village with an incorruptible saint, they chose the fountain.

With the village shuttered, all sleeping except for the feral cats lapping from the fountain, who've now slunk away, she slips her sandals off, hikes her skirt, and wades into the pool. Spray plasters her blouse, she opens the buttons, her wet breasts gleam. He watches her standing with her throat arched back, and he's glad they've come here for however long it lasts.

"Maybe we needed to feel foreign," she told him in the café, "to find a place where there's no way to be anything but strangers."

"Have you ever had the feeling that you've become a stranger to yourself?" he asked.

"Could be a step in the right direction," she told him.

Last night, he walked barefoot down a cobbled street, wearing a suit, a beautiful suit, no shirt, and carrying a cheap suitcase that clumsily resisted the powerful wind, though his body did not. He was going to the ferry even though he realized that in the distance the glittering ocean was actually the moon-glanced tile roofs of the other mountain village. Still, he proceeded until he gradually woke to her sucking his cock, and far off a dog barking, and they rose and opened the shutters and she braced herself against the sill while he entered her from behind, both of them lost in billowing white curtains, while she repeated, *Don't stop*, and he wondered what dream she'd awakened from and if she, too, had lain in the dark thinking that they have to keep fucking because they are afraid of where they might find themselves if they stop.

He watches her and wonders how, when the village wakes to the familiar greetings of roosters and doves, it would appear to those born here to find her spray-drenched, half bare, waist-deep in the swirl, a stranger among the age-old, bare-breasted nymphs, pouring out their bottomless urns. Her arms are graceful like theirs, and for the moment, her eyes, like theirs, seem fixed upon some mystery only she can see.

"Look!" a child shouts. "The nymphs have come to life!" A crowd gathers in the square around the fountain. It's not an apparition of the Virgin, but miraculous enough, and the villagers are ready for their village to have a miracle, too. Let the village below have their saint. Here, where marble has become flesh and blood, it's time to welcome the return of the ancient deities.

But the nymphs are in no hurry for a reunion with mankind. They continue to bathe, staring off, detached from mortal life, unconcerned even as the fissured walls collapse and torrents flood the street, tumbling down the thousand steps, a waterfall that sends the men from the village below rushing into their cathedral, and carrying out their incorruptible saint, hoisted above their heads, while they pray aloud in an old dialect they remember but no longer understand—that no one, perhaps not even God, still understands.

Wash

In a slip that is the only thing pink about the day, she strains from the décolletage of a third-story window. Rain beats her with an intensity reserved for glass while she reels in the pulley line hand over hand, a shoulder strap down, a breast nearly slipping free as clothespins drop from between her teeth, just before she disappears into white furls, fighting in the sheets as the L streams by with its cargo of eyes.

All you'll ever know of her is what you've already learned about hanging out wash.

Vista di Mare

In Genoa, as she packs to leave, he tells her that he doesn't want it to end, and she replies that if he really knew what he wanted, she wouldn't be leaving.

Alone, he continues on along the coast to Rome, and beyond Rome, to Sicily, with no particular destination in mind. Each day there's another train schedule to unriddle, another line to stand in, another crowd to wait among. He's no longer traveling to get somewhere. He's bought a rail pass and is going places in order to ride the trains, to sit, if he can, in an empty compartment where he'll slide down a window and let the gust of racing through Italy blow in his face. From a bench in a crowded station while announcements blare, or from a seat in a train whose rocking makes his handwriting look like a stranger's, he composes a letter to her, as one might write a page in a journal. Back when they first met, they exchanged love letters, which they both have saved. The letters he writes to her now that she's left him in Italy are about the places they meant to discover together, small towns whose names he's given up memorizing, descriptions of weather, scenery, the food they'd meant to share. He writes to her each day, and each night in some new cheap hotel room by a train station he throws the letter away.

And then one day he declares a holiday from letter writing. He doesn't bother to record sleeping beneath a crucifix for the first time since he was a child visiting his Catholic grandmother. He doesn't describe the only hotel available—a converted convent—or how at five a.m., when the bells tolled in the steeple beside his narrow window, it sounded as if waiters carrying metal trays of glass dishes were crashing down flights of stairs. He woke, momentarily confused as to where he was, to the scent of incense from what must have been a mass, mixed with the smell of calamari frying in the kitchen. He doesn't mention how he walked in the rain to the train station past trees that had assumed the same hunched posture as the street musicians who refused to stop playing. He doesn't tell her that his mind is full of the melodies of what presumably are love songs whose names and lyrics he doesn't know. A day goes by without his writing down a single word about all he's seen. That night he has nothing to throw away.

He declares the next day a holiday as well, and that morning he boards a train without so much as looking at a schedule, and then, at a stop where a field of sunflowers overlooks the sea, he impulsively disembarks. Across the tracks sunflowers border a vista where fishermen in red wooden boats work their nets.

He sets off hiking to a town carved into the cliff face, along a trail that climbs through olive and lemon groves and steeply terraced vineyards. After she'd left him in Genoa, he had reduced his belongings to what fit in a backpack. He sweats under its straps and imagines this is how it would have felt to tour Europe when he was young. The year he'd graduated from college, he had a girlfriend who wanted to travel together. Her name was Paulette—a wonderful adventurous girl, whose dorm room was decorated with posters of palm-fringed foreign coasts whose bleached-white houses overlooked indigo water. After making love, her idea of pillow talk was planning trips. He wanted to go with her but was afraid it would seem like more of a commitment than he felt ready for, and when an internship in an advertising firm was offered, he took that instead. Paulette joined the Peace Corps and went off to Africa, and he never heard from her again.

Along a rocky cliff, he stops to watch the gulls soar in the updrafts. He has always tried to remember that through no accomplishment of his own, in this war-torn, exploited, impoverished, unfair world he has enjoyed the relative privilege of being born an American, and now he feels guilty, self-indulgent to regret decisions made in his youth. He's never regarded himself as a regretter. A line from a philosophy course he took back in college comes to him: *Life can only be understood backwards, but it must be lived forwards.* He wonders if he's ever known what he's most wanted. Then it comes to him with a force like tears that for once at least he does know: he wants this, to be here now, climbing with his belongings on his back; he wants this moment of looking out to sea.

The town, etched into the mountainside, is terraced like the vineyard. The streets corkscrew in turns of cobbled steps. He wants to stop here where nothing seems out of sight of the sea, but at a café he's told the only pensione is closed due to a death in the family. The waiter who speaks some English knows of an inexpensive apartment for rent, but doesn't know if the man would like it. Americans, the waiter says, don't feel that they're on holiday unless they have a *vista di mare.* That's why the available apartment is so inexpensive.

"What does it look out on?" he asks.

"*Cipressi,*" the waiter says.

"*Non capisco,*" he says.

"Cypress trees."

Voyeur of Rain

Three stories above the alley, Marty steps onto the back porch for a smoke. He's down to three—morning, afternoon, evening. Clouds smolder above the roofs. The ring of church bells blocks away sounds diffused by the misting drizzle. It's been overcast for weeks, a time during which Marty has come to feel increasingly indistinct. Across the gangway between apartment buildings, a lightbulb softly illuminates a bathroom window. Someone, also indistinct, has stepped into a shower.

As Marty watches, the distorted, fragmented reflections on the marbled glass reassemble into momentary glimpses of a woman. She doesn't know he's watching. If she did, it would alarm her even though he can see no more than the blurred flesh tone of her back as she turns closer to the pane. It's an opaque window, as open to the public gaze as the weathered brick wall it's set in, and yet, on the other side of the glass, the hint of a woman showering makes a bathroom light intimate. Probably there were once plastic curtains, but now it appears the water from her shower must be jetting against the inside of the pane and splashing off a tiled sill. He imagines the steam rising around her as a downpour flattens her hair and rivulets pour down glass, tile, skin, down her legs, puddling at her bare feet before swirling into a gurgling drain.

If, rather than a misting drizzle, the force of her shower

pummeled the city, flooding the gutters and swirling into echoey sewers, Marty wouldn't be standing out here. Along the streets the blurred shapes of pedestrians like a population of mourners under stately black umbrellas would pass silently through fuming exhausts and the distorted beams of vaporish headlights. Marty would have cracked opened his back door and, rather than venturing onto the porch, he'd have exhaled the day's last smoke through the sieve of a rusted screen door studded with droplets. He wouldn't be aware of the nearness of her nakedness. He'd be a voyeur only of the shape-shifting rain.

Above the alley, a gray squirrel tightroping along a slick black phone line sends perched starlings skyward. Marty wonders if it's the same squirrel that has managed through death-defying gymnastics to visit his bedroom windowsill each morning, lured there by the stale peanuts Marty sets out. The peanuts were stale from the start. Marty bought a bag of them from a blind vendor who had been guided by his muzzled pit bull to the steaming grate of a subway. Marty could hear the trains rushing below and feel their vibrations rising through his soles. He dropped loose change into the coffee can stuffed with dollar bills and as he took a bag of peanuts from the vendor's hand, Marty wasn't sure whether he'd misheard the man. He didn't bother to ask, "Pardon?" and simply said, "Thank you," and walked away, but in a voice scrambled by the updraft of trains, it sounded as if the vendor had said, "God bless, asshole."

Perhaps he'd said, "God bless your soul."

The nuts were stale and tasted of mold, but rather than pitch them, Marty set two peanuts on his windowsill each evening before going to sleep. In the morning he'd wake to see the squirrel nibbling one of the nuts on the sill. The other nut the squirrel took to bury.

"Top of the morning to you, little fellow," Marty would say, his first words of the day—sometimes his only words.

A couple of nights ago, Marty realized he was out of peanuts. That next morning—actually in the semidark before morning—he was awakened by a voice in a dream whispering, "Awake, asshole." The words were spoken at the same pitch as the scrape of claws shredding the window screen. At first light, Marty could see the silhouette of what appeared to be a flying squirrel affixed to the screen. Its yellowed rodent teeth were gnawing into Marty's room. He had never noticed, until he saw the underside of the squirrel clinging to his screen, how closely squirrels resemble rats.

Instead of buying more nuts to dole out, or finally opening an ancient box of Cracker Jack—the box he had stolen from a burning candy store when he was a child (a fire Marty sometimes wonders if he set), a singed box of Cracker Jack carried with him ever since from place to place—Marty decided the time had come to stop feeding the squirrel. The following night he dreamed that rats had invaded his apartment. They wanted to pick out his eyeballs as if they were nut meats in a broken shell, one eye to eat and one to bury, and all that prevented them from doing so were the tears he wept. He woke in moonlit darkness to a pillow soaked in either sweat or tears. The squirrel was spread-eagled again, furiously scratching and gnawing at the screen. Marty latched the window and pulled the shade. He had enjoyed the fresh breeze at night, and now the small apartment felt even more confining. But Marty has run out of reasons to leave. There's no longer a pay phone at the subway station that he would walk to in order to call in sick. The pay phones have disappeared overnight and Marty doesn't have a cell. Even if he did, he can't remember what number to call.

Through the marbled glass of the bathroom window

aglow three stories above the alley, none of the city is visible: not the squirrel sashaying along a wire, or the birds lifting into smoldering sky, or black roofs shiny with drizzle, or the man standing across the gangway, flicking the meteor of a cigarette over the railing. The woman in the shower has squeezed shampoo into the palm of her hand and works it to a lather in her brunette hair. Her arms, slender and graceful, rise above her head as she massages the shampoo into suds, and then she ducks her head beneath the drumming water. Suds stream down her steaming body. She has turned directly toward him. In a downpour, her cupped hands lather her small breasts.

Naked

"You're going to leave your watch on?" she asks him, as if he's guilty of an indignity on the order of disrobing down to all but his socks.

"You're leaving on your cross?"

It's not a question he'd have otherwise asked, especially given the way the cross—gold, delicate, and too tiny to crucify a God larger than an ant—brushes the pale slope of her left breast.

"If you're leaving on your Old Spice," she says.

"If you're leaving on your mascara," he says.

"If you're leaving on your road-rash whiskers," she says.

"And then there's your gypsy earrings."

"I've put them in the wineglass," she says.

"But you've left the holes in your earlobes behind."

"And what about your beeper?" she asks.

"Long gone."

"Not if I can still hear it beeping in my mind, in my sleep, in my . . ."

"Fine. I'll take care of it," he says, "once you do the same with your concealed weapon."

"First take off that wire," she says.

"I will if you'll remove that birthmark."

"It's a tattoo!"

"A tattoo. Of what?"

"Dark matter."

"Hearts are out of fashion?"

"And when were you intending to take off that paper yarmulke?" she asks.

"It's male pattern baldness," he says. "My father's began that way. In certain indoor lighting I'd think he was sprouting a halo."

"As long as it isn't tonsure," she says.

"As long as we're on the subject," he says, "I'd really appreciate it if you'd remove that sinister, androgynous hand puppet."

"You mean 'ambidextrous,' right? Because if there's one thing Lil' Martin is not, it's 'androgynous.' And if Lil' Martin goes, you have to lose the parrot. I don't care how sensitive, needy, jealous, and neurotic, not to mention obscene, it can get."

"*Pieces of eight! Pieces of eight! You piece of shit vindictive bitch!*"

"See what I mean?" she says.

"Well, so long as we're on the subject, sweetheart, I've been meaning to mention that I didn't appreciate it when your mother asked if I'd ever trained as a ventriloquist."

"She was merely making conversation."

"And darling, I wasn't going to bring this up either, but since we're being candid there're the hair extensions, and the nail extensions, the braces, the Liz Taylor violet contacts, the disconcerting shadow of—"

She interrupts, "And I wasn't going to bring up the full Groucho, but please, please, please," she pleads, "even if I laughed at first, it's not funny anymore, especially when you pick me up at the airport or we go out to dinner or a party. Darling, I swear I'll strip off anything and everything to get intimate beyond your wildest fantasies if you'll just remove that ludicrous Groucho."

"My love, what Groucho?"

Tea Ceremony

The tentative first snow has become a ticking sleet that despite its bone-chill looks molten in the streetlights. Their shoes—his high-tops, her purple suede boots—are soaked from the quest he's led them on, up one slushy block and down another, since they were asked to leave the movie theater.

"Are we lost yet?" Gwen asks.

"Nothing looks the same in the snow. I swear there's this neat coffeehouse with a woodstove around here," Rick says. "I found it by smell last time."

"If it's someplace you used to go with Hailey, let's forget it. Being there would feel creepy to me," Gwen says.

"You think I'd drag us around freezing because I'm looking for a place I'd been to with someone else?"

"You're right, you wouldn't want to violate the sacred memory."

"Jeez, you're in a shitty mood. If you think it's my fault getting us kicked out, I apologize."

"I was in a great mood. What's more romantic than getting eighty-sixed for public lewdness and stepping into the first snow of the year? I loved walking in it together. Who drew a snow heart on the window of a car, and who walked away before we could write in our initials?"

"Sorry, I was freezing. I'm not dressed for this. I need to

keep moving," Rick says. "Look, there's something open. We're saved."

The restaurant's windows are steamed opaque. Inside, an illegible sign diffuses pink neon across the slick plate-glass window and the Formica counter. There's a scorched, greasy griddle smell. The few customers at the counter, all men, eat with their coats on. Beyond the counter are four empty Formica tables.

"I want to go on record that I have never been in this place before," Rick says. "Nor will I ever be in this place again with anyone but you."

"You say that now."

"I'd never be able to find this place again if I wanted to."

"How about by smell?"

They sit at the table farthest from the counter and wedge their chairs together to study the plastic menu. Gwen opens her Goodwill fur coat and Rick unbuttons his Levi's jacket, but like the people at the counter, they keep their coats on. An overweight waitress in a food-stained white uniform, her face ruddy with broken capillaries, shuffles over on swollen legs to take their order. The waitress waits, regarding them through eyes outlined in tarry mascara. *Sandra* is stitched in red on her uniform above the droop of her considerable bosom.

"You kids need more time?"

"I think I'll have hot tea instead of coffee," Gwen tells Rick. "Can I just get a tea?" she asks the waitress.

"Sure can, hon," Sandra says.

"Tea sounds right for the weather," Rick says. "This may be another first. I don't think I ever ordered tea in a restaurant."

"What about a Chinese restaurant?" Gwen asks.

"That doesn't count," Rick says. "You don't order. It just comes."

"So, two teas?" the waitress asks.

"Two hot teas."

"That it? Nothing to eat?"

"Crumpets, maybe," Rick says. "Do you have crumpets?"

The waitress isn't amused.

"Just the tea, please," Gwen tells her.

"You got it, hon," the waitress says, and writes down the order on her pad. "You want cream or lemon?"

"Lemon," Gwen says, "I'd love some lemon."

"Lemon for me, too," Rick says.

The waitress writes it down.

"How about some honey?" the waitress asks her. "We got these little breakfast honeys for toast I could bring you."

"Thank you so much," Gwen says, smiling at Sandra, "just lemon's fine."

"She an old friend of yours, hon, a long-lost aunt, or maybe a fairy godmother?" Rick asks after the waitress shuffles off.

"She's just being nice. She seems lonely. She's probably the only woman in here most of the time. Maybe I remind her of someone."

"Remind her of who?"

"How should I know? A daughter she never had. Or one she did, a love child who ran away from home and every time the door here opens Sandra thinks it might be her prodigal finally coming back."

"That would explain why she doesn't consider me a worthy escort. You notice the evil eye I was getting."

"Maybe she could see I'd been crying. Can you tell?"

"You look like you just came in from the cold."

Gwen polishes a teaspoon with a paper napkin and examines her reflection in the concave finish. "My eyes are puffy," she says.

Rick takes the spoon from her, brings it to his lips as if it's brimming with steaming soup, and sips. "I love the taste of your reflection," he says, dropping his voice. "I could lick it off mirrors."

"A little over the top, but better. You're making a come-back," Gwen says, and takes his hand and slides it into the pocket of her fur coat. The strapless bra Rick undid in the movie theater is still balled in the pocket. The pocket has a hole in it and Rick can reach through the pocket and then through the torn lining of the coat to brush his fingers along Gwen's right breast.

"Oh-oh," Rick says, "this is how it started at the movie."

"God, I was so close, too," she says. "I blame it on that old, atmospheric theater and its velvet seats and winking starry sky. Like we'd entered a time machine to get there, the way the movies used to be. I always envied those generations that grew up making out at drive-ins instead of ordering Netflix. I wanted us to come together while Fred and Ginger were dancing."

"Foreplay interruptus," Rick says. "We're both probably suffering from posttraumatic sex disruption. No wonder you got upset about a heart on a car window."

"It wasn't just a *car*. It was a vintage Jaguar. That was the point, a beautiful, sleek green Jag inscribed with a heart. Tomorrow morning some lonely venture capitalist is going to come out and find that heart on his car and see only my initials in it 'cause you were freezing and couldn't wait around. He'll think it was a message for him and inscribe his initials where yours were supposed to be, and then he'll slowly cruise through the city, hoping for *G loves blank space*, whoever she is, to wave as he goes by."

Sandra brings a plastic tray to their table. Arranged on the tray are two small metal pots filled with steaming water and two thick white chipped cups on matching chipped saucers. There are two Salada tea packets on a separate plate, two spoons, and a little white bowl of lemon wedges. She carefully transfers each item to their table, setting a cup, pot, and spoon before each of them, and the bowl of lemon wedges in the middle. She opens each tea packet and places a tea bag in each cup and then from her apron pocket produces two small containers of honey.

"Anything more I can get you?" Sandra asks.

"This is wonderful," Gwen says. "I wasn't expecting a tea ceremony when I ordered."

Sandra smiles, pleased. "It's just tea bags," she says. "My mother really knew how to brew tea—real loose tea from India in a little silver ball with a chain. She'd read the leaves."

"Really!" Gwen says. "I always wanted to see someone do that. My mother told me my Nona Marie used to read the cards. Not tarot, just regular playing cards. The family story is that it was the cards that told my grandmother her future was in America."

"I read the cards," Sandra says. "It's in my family. All the women can do it. My sister Irene can read eggs. Don't laugh," she says to Rick. "It's true. I read palms."

"Who taught you?" Gwen asks. "Or did you just like know how?"

"My mother taught me. She taught me what I already knew but didn't have the confidence for. I can show you," Sandra says, and sits down at their table. She extends her hand toward Gwen, and Gwen releases Rick's hand in the pocket of her fur coat, and gives her hand to Sandra.

"It's amazing what we're born knowing if someone just shows us," Gwen says.

"Yeah, and amazing what we think we know when what we know is nothing," Sandra says. "You have a warm, lovely hand, hon." She turns Gwen's hand palm up and lightly traces the lines with her crooked forefinger, studying them, and then looking up at Gwen, who meets Sandra's eyes and smiles.

Sandra doesn't smile back.

"You're laughing on the outside, but your heart is crying," Sandra says.

Rick feels caught off guard. He notices Gwen flinch and

instinctively draw back, but Sandra grips her wrist. Gwen closes her hand and Sandra gently pries it back open and studies it again. "You two, you're the wrong chemicals to mix," she says, and shakes her head disapprovingly.

"Pardon?" Gwen says.

"Not a good fit, no balance. Don't go near the ledge together," Sandra says, and pushes herself up as if she's suddenly weary, then shuffles away.

"Mondo weirdo," Rick says. "There goes her tip. I think we just experienced the gypsy tea ceremony. That line about crying in your heart sounds like it comes out of *Fortune-telling for Dummies*."

He pours hot water over his tea bag; the water in the cup turns tannic.

"My great-aunt Lucile used to look like she was reading tea bags," he tells Gwen. "She'd put hot tea bags on her eyes when she had a migraine. She could tell the future from the spatters of bacon fat, too, and forecast winners at the track from feeling the fuzz on a raspberry."

He sips his tea. The water that appeared to be hot is tepid.

Gwen reaches for the glass container of sugar that huddles together with the salt and pepper shakers, a squeeze bottle of mustard, a bottle of Tobasco, and a clotted bottle of catsup missing its cap around the napkin dispenser, like a little village rising from a Formica plain.

"Did you and your friends ever fill the sugar container with salt when you were in high school?" Rick asks.

"What a callow, guy thing to do," Gwen says. She stops before pouring sugar into her cup, and instead touches the tip of her index finger to the sugar spout and then extends the sugary finger toward Rick. "Taste. Some gang of knuckleheads like your high school homies might have been messing around here."

"It's sweet," Rick says. He licks the grains from her fingertips, then spreads her middle and forefinger as if spreading her legs and runs his tongue down the side of her forefinger to the webbing and laps her there. She takes his hand, sprinkles sugar on his forefinger, guides it to her lips, and sucks it. He closes his eyes.

"Did you like it in the movie theater?" Gwen asks.

"Loved it. I'm sorry we got kicked out into the cold before we found out if we could get off before Fred at least gets to kiss Ginger."

"What if going to that old theater was going back in the past, and because we got kicked out instead of staying until it was over and returning to the present, we were kicked out into the past? I mean, look at this place. Think about outside, how nothing looked the same." Gwen releases his hand and bobs her tea bag in the cup. The string slips from the staple that attaches the bag to the Salada label, and she spoons the tea bag out and presses it to her eye. "Oooh, that feels good. Great-Aunt Lucile was on to something." Gwen places the tea bag on her saucer, and then sprinkles sugar on the lemon wedges in the bowl. "I like tart tastes. I used to suck lemons even when I was a little kid. My friends all thought I was crazy. I like how clean they make my mouth feel." She sucks at a lemon wedge, and then inserts the wedge into her mouth and retracts her lips, giving Rick a lemon-peel smile.

He peels open a honey container, dabs out a fingertip of honey, outlines her lips, and kisses her. The lemon wedge still in her mouth blocks the probing of his tongue. Her kiss tastes of lemon oil. He dabs his forefinger in the honey again, and then slips his hand beneath the table and carefully slides it between the folds of her fur coat and up under her heather woolen skirt. When he reaches her thighs, her legs part. She looks at him and narrows her eyes. There's the tink of her spoon as her right hand absently stirs her tea. "So you think maybe we're like stranded in the past together?" Rick asks. The lemon peel smiles back at him from between her lips. The radiant warmth of her body defies the grains of ice slashing through the dark trees that line the curb, the sleet ticking against the pinkish plate-glass window and pocking the film of snow on the windshields of parked cars. No way would that heart on the Jag survive until morning. She slouches down in her chair, pressing his sticky fingertip against her panties, and then past the elastic so that the honey mixes with her slickness. They may have entered the past, but for this moment there's only the present between them.

From behind the counter, Sandra locks them in a nonstop stare.

With his free hand, Rick raises his teacup to his lips. Gwen's eyes are closed, she's breathing heavier, nostrils flared and her lips parted, revealing a silent lemon-yellow sigh. When she slides toward his finger so that it enters, Rick whispers, "We can't let on we're from the future. They don't want our kind here. Sweetheart, you have to at least make like you're sipping your tea."

The Question

A mime is climbing stairs. He climbs reluctantly, each leaden step an act of resignation, which may explain why, despite his effort, he's not ascending. He no more wants to reach the top than a man mounting another kind of stage—a platform where an executioner stands waiting with an ax.

Or perhaps the executioner is seated in a portable director's chair, puffing through a slit in his hood the cigarette meant for the condemned while stropping the blade of a guillotine that has just failed the cabbage test.

Or perhaps the stairs lead to a hangman tying a knot with the care that his wife expended just that morning braiding their daughter's hair.

The mime climbs and climbs, but cannot conquer the three-step flight that peaks in the space reserved for him in the mercy seat.

Or perhaps . . . but wait!

There's been an error in interpretation. The mime isn't climbing. All along he's been marching in place. Still, from his body language, not to mention the look engraved on his face, it's clear that misinterpretation is not to be confused with a stay of execution.

Okay, then the mime is *marching*—marching down a buzzing, fluorescent corridor in the bowels of a prison, toward a gurney for an operation that requires only an anesthesiologist and a chaplain.

He is marched at dawn across a deserted square to a send-up of pigeons, and takes his place against the riddled wall that faces an unshaven, disheveled firing squad. Their hungover master of ceremonies, a captain, smelling of women, stands sipping menudo from a Dunkin' Donuts coffee cup, sheepishly aware that he has just smoked the cigarette prop. Instead of a sword, the captain raises a blood-red parasol that theatrically pops open. Instead of a sidearm to deliver the coup de grâce, he's holstered a cell phone that is carrying on its own nonstop, one-way, outraged conversation. As for the blindfold, well, each member of the audience seems to be wearing it. On further inspection, each soldier in the firing squad is wearing one, too. And yet, despite the disordered proceedings, and just before the *Ready, aim*, etc., command, the captain remembers to ask, "Any last words?"

Transients Welcome

Old Man Martin checks into a cheap hotel to die. He winks when the Desk Clerk asks how long he'll be staying, but the Desk Clerk mistakes that to mean he should send up a woman. The woman doesn't notice the old man's haggard expression, his pallor, his jaundiced eyes. What she's alert to is the man lovingly slipping his belt out of the loops of his trousers or studying her scars with too much fascination.

"What you here for?" Martin asks, his voice the backside of a cough.

"Come for sex," the woman says as if sharing a confidence. She's not a native speaker.

"Say what?" Martin yells, as if she's the one who's deaf.

"Come for sex."

"Comfort the sick? You a doctor? I don't want no more doctors."

"Pesos, hole," the woman says, keeping it elementary, gesturing that *hole* includes her flabby breasts.

"Soul? What'll you pay? You the devil?"

"Hole!" she says, and strips off her maid's smock.

Old Martin breaks into a demented grin. "The whole enchilada? Know the price of the whole enchilada? Holy moley!" He collapses on the bed, laughing like a lunatic, chanting, "Holy, holy, holy moley," and drubbing the mattress with his heels and fists so that the bedsprings squeal like they're doing it, and the picture of the ghost ship emerging from a fog of dust sails from the nail above the headboard to the floor.

"You holy, holy loco?" the woman shouts, and throws up her hands.

"Hole? You the grave digger?" Martin sits up cradling an air guitar. *You can dig my grave with a bloody spade*, he sings in a rasp befitting of Blind Boy Martin. *Oh, Lord, dig my grave with a bloody spade, but just make sure the grave digger gets paid*. He fumbles on his specs—one lens is missing, the other's cracked—and, squinting, fishes a coin from his worn change purse and places it in her outstretched palm. "That why you dressed in mourning?"

"I'm naked," she says.

"You the Dark Angel? Where's your wings?" Martin grabs her arm and tries to claw the coin back from her clenched fist. "Give it up, you damned imposter," he's shouting. "That's my life's savings."

She tears away, slams out the door leaving her smock behind, and races dizzily down the spiral of back stairs, *Holy, holy, holy* looping her brain. She can't say why she's sobbing. The life's savings has seared her fist shut so tightly that she can feel the face stamped on the coin. It's her face, and on the tails side there's a heart, her heart, wreathed in flames like the Virgin's heart in holy pictures. Heat scalds through her veins and renders fleshiness down to sinew. Body supple again, scars erased, lacquered with tears and sweat, she busts out of the sheet-metal door, nearly knocking it off its rusted hinges.

In the alley, men are drinking rotgut between wars. Their rap anthem whines as they debate the day's pack order of has-beens, coulda-beens, and wannabes. They've been one-upping one another's bullshit tales of conquest as if auditioning for the *Poontang Monologues*. Whatever her native tongue, she's had to become fluent in the dialect they speak. They gape as if at an apparition. Before she can whirl back up the stairs, she's tackled. There's no confusion here between whole and hole. They want most what she conceals and when she won't unclench her fist, swearing she can't, one of them smashes a bottle against the banister, and one opens a straight razor, and another slides a bayonet out of a cowboy boot.

Her cries echo and dim along twenty-watt corridors. *Holy, holy, holy.* Old Martin starts from his nap. In his dream of fog and dust was the voice praying so fervently his own? He hugs himself in the nest of soiled sheets. The mattress smells of urine, the pillow of hair. He tries whispering a prayer into the megaphone of an empty water glass, and the water glass fogs, as does the dusty window and bureau mirror. He presses the glass to his ear and hears what's left of his breath awash in a seashell. Out at sea, lost in fog, the ghost ship with its cargo of souls plows toward the lonely ringing of a distant buoy.

The Bellboy stands on the other side of the door pressing a cell phone to his ear. He's a Filipino kid whose bleached hair ponytails from beneath a bellhop's hat. His faded red uniform recalls the hotel's grander days. He looks as if he just might shout, *Call for Philip Morris!* Perhaps, beneath his makeup, the Bellboy is older than he appears to be. The Desk Clerk, who has misinterpreted Old Martin's rejection of the woman, has sent the Bellboy.

"Ahoy?" Old Martin shouts into the water glass as if it's a disconnected rotary phone. There's no dial tone, though the ringing in his ears continues to grow louder.

"*Amor,*" the Bellboy answers, and tries the doorknob. Locked. Locked out is the other side of being locked in. The Bellboy has learned that lesson at every reform school that's reformed him. He's learned it on Rikers Island, and learned it again here, where working has resembled explicating a trope: the body is a hotel. Transients enter, becoming guests. Until they arrived, the Bellboy was unaware of all his vacancies. He thought there was only one room available. When the deadbeat guests refused to leave, it became obvious there were other, secret rooms. Instead of checking out, the guests moved down a corridor lit by a red EXIT sign and lined with unnumbered rooms that didn't require keys or maid service; rooms that call for Philip Morris. The closer to the EXIT sign, the smokier and smaller the rooms, until they are too narrow for anything but bedbugs, an ashtray of butts, and a single guest who lies with his arms crossed over his chest, puffing smoke rings through a whistling hole in his throat.

"*Amor*," the Bellboy murmurs, ringed by a smoky fog as if he is swinging a censer, like an altar boy in a surplice of incense. "*Amor*," and a voice behind the door answers, "*Amen*."

"More? I'll give you what I got, just stop dinging that bell," Old Martin says into the water glass. He unclasps his change purse and extracts the rosary he was saving to braid through his fist. What use is a rosary now that the coin he was saving to light a vigil candle has been stolen? On his side of the door, Martin inserts the cross like a key into the keyhole, and works the beads out behind it.

The Bellboy drops to his knees and cups his hands. If not a miracle, then a rosary worming from a keyhole is, at least, a metaphor. A rosary begins and ends with a cross. Fingertips trace the beads as if treading the Via Dolorosa from one Station of the Cross to the next. Even in fog you can't be lost once you understand the journey takes you from Station to Station. The Bellboy puts his lips to the keyhole and whispers, "*Gracias*." With his ear beside the keyhole listening for a reply he can hear a muffled bong of clappers, a window imploding, and the thud of a body reeling against the walls. The bells of St. Martin de Porres, the looted church across the street, haunted by a priest said to have hanged himself after being accused of molestation, are tolling.

Kneeling beside the broken water glass, Old Martin, his head pounding apart with each concussion, plugs his ears. On the back stairs the Bellboy has arrived at another Station of the Cross: the Maid, scourged, her throat peeled back like sliced liver. When he covers her with his velvet jacket and braids the rosary into her hair, the severed hand beside her opens to offer him a coin. He would refuse it were it not stamped with his face on one side and a cross on the other. Shivering, his guts cramped, he carries her down the stairs into the furnace room where he sleeps, and slides the spike into his vein, and nods back against the furnace, which clangs through the corroded pipes.

When Old Martin regains consciousness the fog has settled in his chest. Blood is crusted around his nostrils and ears. His battered cardboard suitcase sits unopened on a chair. An envelope has been slipped under his door, a message from the Desk Clerk: Will he be paying the bill for another night?

Better answer yes, Martin thinks, I don't have long, but this might take more time than I figured. He draws the shade like pulling down the night.

Since the Maid vanished and the Bellboy has stopped answering the bell, the Desk Clerk doesn't sleep. Maybe they've absconded together. On top of everything else the furnace has died and the plumbing is backed up, no doubt thanks to the bag lady in 1414—actually 1313 if the hotel allowed unlucky numbers. She claims disability but skates on her walker like a Roller Derby queen through the alleys at night and, contrary to hotel policy, sneaks in strays. The cat litter she's been flushing down the toilet for years has turned to concrete and the hotel is constipated. His bowels feel like concrete, too. The Desk Clerk shakes the bottle of Pepto-Bismol as if he has the bag lady by the throat. He chug-a-lugs, then from the corners of his mouth licks what looks like rabid foam. He was told that when he was a child with a stomachache he called the medicine Pepto-Dismal. His lips have calcified into the grin of a clown.

Too many worries, too much responsibility, and now the Desk Clerk must perform the Maid's and Bellboy's duties as well, and do so with the proper air of dignity so as not to seem to be a Desk Clerk demoted to a lesser office. No labor is as exhausting as that which one feels is beneath him. The buzzing bismuth-pink neon sign that hangs in the lobby window flickers its letters across the Desk Clerk's body: TRANSIENTS WELCOME. Soon the flickery buzz of neon will be the only heat left, he thinks. And that old man who checked in earlier concerns him, as well. He's not as transient as some the Desk Clerk has seen and could be trouble, like that priest who checked in long ago and who continues to reappear, leaving a slick of Extreme Unction. What does the old man want? Not a woman, not a boy.

Recalling the old men from his childhood who gimped along towed by gimpy old mutts, the Desk Clerk unlocks the door to the flyblown Lost and Found. The mutt a deadbeat guest left as collateral has been sleeping there. The Desk Clerk presumes that all who find their way to this hotel are lonely, but the old are lonelier still. He regards the menagerie that Lost and Found has become: a parakeet whose gibberish sounds like a forgotten name, the goldfish with piranha teeth that smiles sardonically as it rises to its fish flakes, the turtle with BUDDY crudely carved into its shell, and the hand-trained flies performing their x-rated aerial show—all emblems of loneliness. The Desk Clerk sends the dog up to the old man.

Were it the old woman he would have sent up a cat— although she probably had one already.

Were it a dog he would have sent up an old man.

There's a logic to the term *EQ* that a manager in the hospitality industry needs to master. What, for instance, would he send a child?

The Desk Clerk's gnawed thumbnail cracks the seal on a fifth of vodka. He pours vodka into the Pepto-Dismal bottle and swishes it around. He's thinking of the children he never had, of children no one wanted, and of his own fatherless childhood. He has become the stepfather of his childhood self. What would he have sent himself that might have changed his life enough so that he didn't end up behind this dead-end desk? When he swallows from the Pepto-Dismal bottle, the vodka tastes pink. He exhales and his breath hangs pinkish over the desk. He's never understood why people say you can't smell vodka. No one claims you can't smell Pepto-Dismal. The conventional wisdom is to send children puppies, kittens, bunnies, hamsters, gerbils. But do animated stuffed animals teach a child the way of the world? Knowing what he knows now, the Desk Clerk would send himself what most terrified him—a spider.

And what would he send a spider?

The question buzzes in his head like an iridescent neon fury trapped between window and shade. He's lived a nocturnal life behind this desk for what? To be rewarded with a demotion to Bellboy? And why? Because in working the night shift, I have relinquished my dreams. Because I have welcomed in phantoms the world pretends are real. Because I have ascribed to cause and effect—believed that diligence results in success, that obsequiousness precedes advancement, consoled myself with proverbs such as: We are all guests in a transient hotel. Because of expedience, because of timidity, because of constipation, because of logic—that misnomer for an utter lack of imagination.

He stands on the desk noosing night in the guise of a phone cord around his windpipe and when he sees the priest blessing him from the doorway of the Lost and Found, the Desk Clerk swings his body off with no excuse other than that he would have sent a spider a trained fly.

Fuses blow. Drains stop up. Upstairs, Old Martin lights

the candle he packed in his suitcase. He suspects it has been night for more than twenty-four hours, but he won't pull up the shade. No one has come to collect. He zips his empty change purse. Does this mean he is through paying bills? He hears paws scratching at the door, a muzzle snuffling, a whimper. He hears the prolonged vowel of a loyal creature that has caught the scent of death.

Martin holds his tin cup over the candle, heating rusty tap water. He takes his used tea bag from the plastic baggie. The night is getting cold. He sets his suitcase on fire and huddles beside it. He lights a smoke from his snuff can of butts and coughs up a taste of green pennies. He's beginning to feel at home.

Flies

It was cool in the Lion House, acrid with the urine of tigers. Roars reverberated like the shouts of kids under a viaduct. The air hummed: flies swarming dung and raw meat. Between the guardrail and cages, zappers grilled in *tzz tzzz* bursts.

"Is there something sweet on the wires?" I asked my father, who was holding my hand as if we were about to cross a busy street.

"No, a light we can't see attracts them."

At each cage I watched, trying to glimpse the light that only flies could see, concentrating on that instant when the flies crackled into the blue sparks that jolted through electric coils into charred piles. A stunned few on their backs propelled in circles through frazzled corpses like tiny motorboats out of control.

"Let's go," my father said, giving my hand a tug, and we stepped out squinting into the sunlight, back on the walkways crowded with Sunday, on our way to see the giraffe, before I realized I'd missed the cats.

Aria

Shhhh . . . you're tipsy, you'll wake up the whole neighborhood.

Shhhh, yourself. And why shush me and not the nighthawks? You think if their squawking doesn't wake people, that I'm going to? Are you implying my voice is more strident?

It's not a fair comparison. Sleepers unconsciously accept nighthawks as part of the night, like crickets.

And we're not like crickets?

Not to the poor sleepers. I remember as a kid waking in the middle of the night to voices laughing or arguing or sometimes singing out on the street. I'd catch snatches of conversation but never enough to figure out who they were or what they were doing up. And I'd lie there envying them having the world to themselves while everybody else slept, until from some window somebody'd yell, "Hey, shut the fuck up!"

See, thanks to us, now you know how the people on the street felt with the night all to themselves. And nobody's even yelled shut the fuck up at us yet.

They will.

You're starting to sound like my mother, except instead of "You'll wake up the neighborhood," she'd say, "You'll wake up the dead." Maybe because we didn't live in a neighborhood. We lived in a 'burb. "You have to be careful," she'd warn me, "women in our family have voices that *project*."

It's a mother's job to make daughters self-conscious.

Actually, she was right, our voices do project. We got them from her. My mother studied voice for years before she got married. She got a scholarship to Oberlin. It's family lore how, when she was valedictorian for her high school class in Grundy Center, Iowa, and got up to give the speech at graduation, the microphone wouldn't work. They had graduations outside, on the football field, and where the end zone ended, farmland began. During her graduation, there was a guy plowing with his tractor, and overhead a crop duster was spraying. My mother had worked on her speech for weeks, and hated it, so she took the broken microphone as an act of God, an omen not to give the speech. Instead, she shrugged at the audience, then threw her head back and belted out an aria—in Italian. She told us that when people congratulated her afterwards, they didn't say it was beautiful, but rather that she could be heard in the next county.

What did she sing?

"Vissi d'arte" from *Tosca*—*I lived for art*. What else? She was seventeen. When she sings in choir I can always hear her voice hovering above all the others. It used to embarrass me as a kid. She was always a little disappointed I didn't go to Oberlin and study voice like her.

I never heard you sing.

You don't recall it, but you did.

I did?

I sang to you in a dream—actually, a nightmare—God! I'd nearly forgotten. Remember that time in Chicago, looking for a bottle of wine at two in the morning? Everything was closed except a few package liquor stores that only sold cheap booze and finally we found a place way on the North Side.

Malek's. On Bryn Mawr. We bought a dusty bottle of champagne.

Right. And when we drove up we thought the place had

just been robbed. There were two squad cars and they had a guy across the hood of one of them.

A Hispanic kid with rolling eyes.

Uh-huh. He looked scared, and whatever they had him for didn't have anything to do with robbing the store. But it reminded you of one time back in college when you were walking toward some L station from a girlfriend's house and you saw the cops working over a kid and suddenly realized it was your best friend from when you were ten years old, in your old neighborhood.

Yeah. Andy Cardona. They'd caught him trying to stick up a gas station on Wilson Avenue. It was weird. They had him in cuffs and getting in the car he looked my way and recognized me, too, and grinned.

Well, about a month after that night when we found the champagne, I had this dream I never told you about: It was night and I was waiting in the car and there was a robbery. I saw two huge guys in ski masks and black leather coats run out carrying guns, and for a second I was terrified they were going to come to the car where I was waiting because I'd seen them, but they changed their minds and kept going, and then I suddenly remembered you'd gone inside to buy us a bottle. I could hear an ambulance wailing and I couldn't seem to get out of the car. To protect me, you'd locked the doors somehow with the key. Blue dome lights from police cars and red lights from ambulances bled over the plate glass. I kept trying to see out the window, which kept fogging with my breath; I kept hoping, waiting for you to come out. The ambulance attendants ran inside. They wheeled someone out under a sheet. I couldn't see who. I watched them drive away. And after that the liquor store sign went out. The street was empty and dark. Suddenly, the locks *pinged* and I could get out of the car. I looked into the window of the dark liquor store just to make sure you weren't there. I didn't know where I was. It was your city, not mine. So I just walked along the streets. It began to snow, but I walked all night and came to your old neighborhood. I recognized it from what you'd told me. There were the Mexican murals and gang graffiti on the walls of viaducts, there was the church with twin steeples where you'd gone to school. There were cars lined in front of the church doors. I went inside. The church was lit by candles, all these candles. Everyone was dressed in black. All the people in your family I'd heard about. I recognized them, your mother in a black veil, your father, your aunts and uncles and cousins, the ones who were priests, the ones who were war heroes or crooks or butchers or drunks, the blessed deserters, none of whom knew anything about me. You were dead but I was the ghost. They were having a funeral mass. The coffin surrounded by candles was in the middle of the aisle and I knelt in the back of the church and then I suddenly couldn't help myself, it was as if the wind was blowing through my body and emerging changed to song. I began to sing this aria I didn't know I knew. It was so beautiful, I remember that, but I don't remember the melody or the language I was singing in. Not English. This tremendously sad sweet song came out of me and filled the whole church and I knew you knew it was me singing for you. Everyone turned toward where I knelt in shadow and listened. And when I was finally finished I walked back outside into the snow. There wasn't anything left for me to do once I knew you'd heard my song.

Belly Button

What was it about the belly button that connected it to the Old Country?

Perhaps Busha's concern for its cleanliness. Those winter bath nights, windows and mirrors steamed as if we were simmering soup, my hands "wrinkled as prunes," the slippery water sloshing as I stepped from the tub into her toweling embrace.

Outside, night billowed like the habits of nuns through vigil lights of snow. Kraków was only blocks away, just past Goldblatt's darkened sign. Bells tolled from the steeple of St. Casimir's, over the water towers and smokestacks, over the huddled villages and ghettos of Chicago.

And at the center of my body, Busha's rosary-pinched fingers picked at that knotted opening that promised to lead inward, but never did.

Ice

They stepped carefully onto the pond as if they were about to walk on water. Its surface was inscribed with a cursive of scars resembling those faintly visible on the daylight moon frosted to a faint blue sky. The farther out they walked, the more flawless the ice became.

"I think we've gone far enough," she said, gazing down, a mittened hand shading her eyes. Wind, nearly unnoticeable so long as they kept moving, blew her hair. "Ice this clear can't be safe."

"It's thicker than you'd suppose," he said.

"Can you feel the pressure of our weight forcing up water? Each step makes the bottom bubble up. You can see the bubbles frothing against the underside of the ice," she said. "Let's go back."

"Those aren't water bubbles," he told her.

"Then what are they?"

"Last summer, during a wedding in the park, after the bride and groom cut the giant palace of a cake, instead of waltzing, they turned their backs on the orchestra and set sail across the pond in a rowboat. They left all their gifts behind except for a Methuselah of champagne that was supposed to be for toasts. It was propped in the stern, poking up like a lopsided chimney on a transatlantic steamer, and the boat listed under its weight, but they'd have made it across the pond if not for a sudden summer storm that blew up and capsized the boat. The bottle, Taittinger, if I remember correctly—I'm never sure how to pronounce it—sank to the bottom. It must have just popped its cork. In our honor."

They walked farther out. The pond wind had a skating quality. It slammed against their calves when she stopped again suddenly. "Oh, my God!" she said. "There's a huge, dark fish rising from the bottom, a giant catfish or a carp, something too big for this pond. Look at it, just beneath us, opening its enormous maw as if to swallow us whole once the ice gives way. I can see its grinning teeth. Please, we must turn back."

"Don't worry, it's not a monstrous fish. It's the distortions in the ice that make it appear to be. At that wedding last summer, during the storm, when the rowboat capsized, the distraught, drunken guests wheeled the concert grand with its black tuxedo finish from the pavilion and down to the pond, and launched it to save the bride and groom. It floated out, but sank before it reached them. It's still submerged, playing Strauss, perhaps. What you thought were teeth is the keyboard."

They walked out farther still. The wind they hadn't noticed on shore felt round, like the pond, resisting their progress even as it pushed them from behind. If not for the pond, there'd have been no awareness of there even being a shore.

"I see a candle flame following us, rising from below like that line of poetry from *Dr. Zhivago* you are so fond of. I can't recall the words exactly, but I see it flickering just below."

"You mean, *It snowed and snowed, the whole world over . . . A candle burned on the table; / A candle burned*? If memory serves, I recited it to you the evening we met. You said it warmed your heart."

"Look! The flame has formed a halo around us, as if we're standing on a frosted windowpane that the candle is about to dissolve."

"But that doesn't happen in the poem. Maybe you're thinking of the movie, which I haven't seen, but in the poem it's *The blizzard sculptured on the glass / Designs of arrows and whorls. / A candle burned . . .*"

"I see a drowned girl veiled in white, holding the candle, and a tiara of flowers is coming apart in her flowing hair. We have to go back!"

"But we're perfectly safe. The ice is two feet thick." He began to jump up and down to make his point, rising higher with each jump as if the ice had the spring of a trampoline, and landing harder and harder on his boot heels.

Beneath them the ice began to shudder. Jets of froth obscured the clarity as if a fuming fissure had opened at the collapsing bottom of the pond. Giant flukes and whorled flame conflated, enmeshed in veils of milky froth. A rumble boiled to a thunderous crescendo, the sound of cracks shooting through ice like jagged lightning through a summer storm. She screamed and turned to run.

"Wait, wait, don't move," he called after her.

She slipped and went down in a graceful slow motion, then slid back up at hyperspeed and kept running.

"It's only a train," he shouted over the roar.

Far off, on the other side of the pond, behind a scrim of skeletal trees, the scuffed silver salt-stained train arrowed across a metal trestle.

"It must be some weird echo," he yelled. "Not a Doppler effect, but there's no doubt a scientific name for it that we'd recognize if we were as up on acoustical engineering as we are on Russian poetry."

She went down again hard, ungracefully this time, crawled back to her feet, and kept going. To watch her was like seeing, from the perspective of consciousness, someone struggling to run in a dream.

He caught up to her at the edge of the pond. She stepped

onto the bank and when she turned to look back, her face was streaked with tears. It was the first time he'd seen her cry. Her salt tears had pitted the freshwater ice and left a trail. Wasn't it she who had told him, shortly after they met, that in every relationship there's always one person who scatters a trail of bread crumbs for the other to follow? He'd written it down in a notebook where he kept quotes he wanted to remember from books he'd read.

"I'm sorry it upset you," he said. "I thought you might like walking out on the ice together. It's so quiet now in winter, the summer buskers and crowds all gone, the band instruments hibernating in their cases, musical shapes like the pavilion muffled in snow, the organ grinder and his neon-green monkey migrating south like the songbirds—it's too cold for a spider monkey. Just us, walking across a pond as peacefully as if we were walking across the daylight moon."

"I saw a dead girl holding a candle and staring up through the ice, and she looked like me," she said. "She looked like me enough to be me. As if the ice were a mirror."

"Well, she wasn't you. You can't be both dead and alive any more than you can be in two different places at once."

"I can be in two places if I am in two different times."

"But you're here now with me in this time."

"Who knows for how long? Someday I may be looking back on being in love, and which me will be more real?"

"And who said the girl, if there was a girl, was dead? More likely is that she's only sleeping in a cryogenic state of suspended animation. I'll go back and wake her with a kiss."

"She's under two feet of ice."

"It's so transparent she'll feel the impression of warmth on her lips."

"I wouldn't if I were you, she'll break through the ice and pull you under."

"Nonsense," he said, "I'll be back in a jiff."

He started out across the pond again, retracing the pitted trail of her tears. From way out, he turned to smile and wave, but if she was there at all, he could no longer distinguish her from the background of winter.

The Story of Mist

Mist hangs like incense in the trees. Obscured trains uncouple in a dusk that is also obscured, and later, a beacon sweeps across the faces of a crowd gathered at the shoreline, standing knee-deep in mist.

In a corrugated shed lit by a misty overhead bulb, a welder working late looks up from acetylene, then removes his mask to kiss his wife, who's brought him a cold beer.

Smoke smolders through the projection beam as if the old theater is filling with mist; on-screen, gigantic faces gaze out at an audience of shadows.

He holds her to him with his left arm, extending the blue flame away from them with his right, and she holds the foaming bottle of beer away from them as if it, too, were a torch. When their mouths touch, her breath enters him like mist.

An endless chain of boxcars slams back together with a sound of rolling thunder, thunder smothered by mist.

She can see the mist rising from the hairs along his skin, and touches him as carefully as she might draw a straight razor along the length of his body.

Listen, in the dead of night, high above the mist, steeple-jacks are nailing up the new day's Christ.

A buoy tolls in the mist like the steeple of a little neighborhood church that has drifted out to sea.

A freighter, sounding a melancholy horn, hoists the moon, which it's been towing, from a moonlit slick, and tows it through the mist.

Happy Ending

The only one to arrive fashionably late for the Mogul's little soirée was the last of several rain-soaked bike-delivery kids bringing up Thai takeout. By midnight, the rain had turned into an unexpected, fluorescent snowfall wafting past the windows facing Central Park, and the dozen or so members of the show who'd been invited to the Mogul's suite at the Carlyle had nearly drunk their way through a case of Dom Pérignon. When no one moved to open the last bottle, the Mogul popped it himself.

"To the success of *EverAfter*," he said. "By the way, that fucking title's got to go."

Everyone raised their flutes and drank.

"I can order up more bubbly," the Mogul said, "but it won't be the same great year."

"Man, they're all great years," said Nestor, the musical director, and drank to that.

"Some are decidedly better than others," the Mogul said. "That's what you pay for."

Nestor bowed, corrected. They'd all witnessed, earlier in the day, what disagreeing with the Mogul could cost.

The Mogul had flown in from L.A. that morning in his private jet to watch the rehearsal. Wearing smoke-gray aviator glasses as if he had piloted the plane himself, he slipped into the theater unannounced and sat silently smoking in the back row. The cast didn't need the smell of cigarillo to know he was there. Gil had never seen the actors more jumpy. Even Renee Wilde and Tony Kayne—TK—the romantic leads, both with established careers, appeared nervous. They'd been working on the play for over a year.

No one called the Mogul "the Mogul" to his face. The nickname wasn't meant affectionately; it alluded to his reputation for being egotistical and ruthless. But it wasn't solely his reputation that put the cast on edge. The rehearsal was a make/break audition. If he liked what he saw, the Mogul was set to buy the film option and help bankroll the dramatic production. If *EverAfter* went on to Broadway, he would buy it outright for a film; and, if that happened, even the writers with their mere 1 percent shares would score.

"You'll never have to teach again, Gil," was how Liam, the director, put it.

EverAfter was a sequence of three one-act plays, each by a different playwright, and unified by a musical score and by the ensemble of actors. Over the course of the evening the audience watched the players changing identities and aging as the stories moved from youth to middle age to maturity. Gil had written the first act, "Youth."

It was set in a haunted jazz club that back in the Roaring Twenties had been a speakeasy, and told the story of an affair between a coked-up chanteuse named Bea and a young trumpet player named Dex. Bea believed Dex was a reincarnated Bix Beiderbecke and that in their former lives, when they'd been lovers, she'd been responsible in a way she could no longer remember for his mysterious death at twenty-eight. Now, back together in love again, Bea feared their fate would repeat itself.

"Dick Jokes," the second act, involved a banjo-picking woman comic touring the Deep South during the Nixon-Kennedy presidential campaign. When "Dick Jokes" ended, the Mogul signaled for a break. He didn't return for an hour, and this time he sat close to the stage next to Liam, who, besides directing, had conceived of *EverAfter* and assembled the cast.

Everyone in the company knew that the third act, "Viste di Mare," had problems. Jeremy Spada, who'd written it, had disappeared into a Mexican alternative medicine clinic, the rumor was with AIDS-related cancer. The act told the story of a couple trying to save their marriage of twenty years by taking a honeymoon cruise on the Adriatic. It opened in the ship's lounge during a storm at sea, with the Captain sitting down at the piano and singing "Slow Boat to China." Sven Nystrom, a noted Shakespearean actor, played the Captain. Halfway through the song, the Mogul interrupted. "Stan," he said, "hold on a sec."

Sven continued to sing until the Mogul stood and raised his voice: "Stan!"

"It's Sven," Sven Nystrom said.

"You're doing it like Sinatra," the Mogul said.

"Actually, Tony Bennett," Sven said. "The Captain's Dutch, but he's always wanted to be an American crooner. You'll see that everyone on this cruise is acting out a fantasy."

"Try it like he thinks he's Michael Jackson," the Mogul said.

"He's *Dutch*. White, retirement age. Why would he want to be something so outlandish as Michael Jackson?" Sven asked.

"Maybe because the corny-white-lounge-singer shtick's already been done to death. Here, have him put these on," the Mogul said, handing his aviator shades up to Sven.

"Wouldn't dark glasses be more Stevie Wonder?" Sven asked, taking the glasses and looking to Liam for support, but all Liam said was, "Nestor, take it from the start of 'China.'"

Sven sat down at the piano, put on the sunglasses, and

resumed singing "Slow Boat to China." He halfheartedly grabbed his crotch a few times à la "Thriller" but still sounded like Tony Bennett.

"Stan," the Mogul called. Sven ignored him and kept crooning.

"Stan!" the Mogul shouted. "Instead of parked on your heinie, you're supposed to be all but moonwalking behind that fucking keyboard."

"It's Sven," Sven said.

"Sorry," the Mogul said, "*Sven*. Do I have that right? Sven, you can deposit those sunglasses on the piano as you leave the stage."

"Pardon me?" Sven asked.

"I have to spell it out? You're toast, Sven," the Mogul said.

Gil was sitting beside Tina Powell, who had written "Dick Jokes." She pulled him toward her so that her lips were beside his ear. "The Mogul just announced that he's bankrolling the show. And that he owns us," she said. "You may never have to teach again."

After the rehearsal, Liam waved Gil over. The Mogul wanted to meet him. "I knew I was going to back the play after I saw your first act, Gil," he said. "Brilliant, spooky stuff. Do you ever write about vampires? The third act totally sucks, though. Can you rewrite it?"

"It's not my play," Gil said.

"I can hire a script doctor," the Mogul said, "but I'd rather someone already connected with our project did it. I'm not even sure I know what the fuck it's supposed to be about. I get the everybody-has-a-fantasy bit, but that's not doing anything for me. Help me out here, Gil. What's there to salvage?"

"The fantasy motif isn't working for you?" Gil asked.

"I'm not Disney, for fuck's sake. You've seen the movies I make. There's got to be something that goes for the throat."

"Passion," Gil said.

"Passion?" the Mogul repeated. "Go on."

"The couple has lost their passion," Gil said.

"Gil, that's brilliant," the Mogul said. "Fucking love it."

"You do? Thanks. I mean it's a little clichéd but—"

The Mogul cut him off. "You know, Gil, a secret to success in this business is to understand there's a fine line between a cliché and a classic, so fine that—not to sound cynical—it's virtually invisible to most people in the audience. You're a classy writer, but you don't let it get in the way of life. Think about a rewrite. Passion. We'll talk more tonight. I'm giving a little soirée."

By the time a second case of champagne arrived, the park trees, ablaze for autumn, were flocked white. Flights of leaves weighted with wet snow gusted through the swirl of flakes as if the park might be stripped bare overnight.

"The wind sounds like whale songs from up here," Tina Powell said. She and Gil stood together at a window, looking out and passing a bottle of champagne between them. "When it comes to beautiful illusions, this city still has a few tricks up its sleeves," Tina said. "Or is that just the booze talking?"

"Makes you want to be out there walking," Gil said.

"Not in these it doesn't." Tina lifted her skirt to give him a better look at her slender calves and violet open-toed pumps. "Wish I'd worn boots."

"Perfect footwear for a soirée," Gil said. "You look lovely tonight."

"Had I known months ago you only flirt when drunk on overpriced bubbly I might have insisted on Petrossian instead of Papaya King," Tina said. "Not that those weren't top New York kosher dogs. When the Mogul makes us rich, we can celebrate. We'll dress our wieners in beluga and get drunk as skunks."

"I'll admit to being a little buzzed maybe, but not drunk," Gil said.

"Too bad. I am, might as well be," Tina said. "What's stopping you? Tonight's a celebration of sorts, no? You'll never have to teach again. You can retire to a hut in Malibu and write that bloodsucker trilogy you've always known you had in you."

A bellman refilled the ice buckets, dimmed the lighting, and asked if he should also clear the food.

"Leave it," the Mogul said, "people are still nibbling." The Mogul had been drinking quietly as if brooding, or maybe his own party bored him. He sat beside an ice bucket as one might sit with a teddy bear, alone on a couch behind a coffee table barricaded with take-out cartons. Take-out cartons occupied almost every surface in the room—the tabletops, the desk, the windowsills. Cartons were balanced on top of other cartons still to be opened. The Mogul rose and began to open some of them, jabbing his chopsticks in for a sample and then re-sealing them.

"Just dipping your beak?" Tina Powell asked.

"Don Fanucci in *The Godfather*," the Mogul answered. "Best line in the movie."

The Mogul explained that when he'd asked for the best Thai delivery in the city, three different restaurants were recommended. They couldn't all be the best, so to settle the question he'd ordered from all three. But now, with the cartons mixed up, it was impossible to tell what had come from where. He had instructed the front desk to send up the delivery boys because he felt the best part of takeout was the ring at the door followed by the smell of steaming food. You knew the food was never as good as it smelled, but it didn't matter. The smell, he said, reminded him of the cheap Asian food he'd survived on when, with no prospects, he hitched his way to L.A., city of dreams, where—young, broke, scuffling, literally picking cigarette butts out of the gutter—he'd determined to make his mark or fucking die trying. In those days when he was always hungry, the food had tasted as good as it smelled.

The Mogul sat back down beside the ice bucket and refilled his glass.

Champagne was being popped all over the room. Debates broke out over what were the best carryout places in the city, Queens against Manhattan, until Liam announced that as far as he was concerned the question wasn't what restaurant was best, but rather, which was most authentic.

"You can say the same thing about theater," Liam said.

TK took that as a cue to tell them all about the time he'd shot a film in Bangkok, and how the food there bore little resemblance to Thai food in New York. He'd especially loved the street food, and never once got sick, at least not from eating. Drink and drugs were another matter. He was partying hard back then. They'd start shooting at six a.m. and he'd clear his head by eating an incendiary curry for breakfast. Lunch was fruit delivered from the great fruit market on Phahonyothin Road: mangoes, young coconuts called *ma praw on*, and fruits TK had never tasted fresh before—mangosteen, jackfruit, lichee. There were fruits he knew only by their Thai names— *lam-yai*, *longkong*—and, speaking of the difference between smell and taste, sometimes a durian, a fruit so putrid-smelling that the hotels posted signs warning it was illegal to bring one inside, yet durians taste like silky custard, like nothing you ever had before. They'd blend them into icy smoothies, and then TK would get a massage from a skinny woman who spoke no English but could cure a hangover by walking her fingers down his spine. He didn't think you could get authentic Thai in New York, though maybe a durian could be found in the wilds of the Bronx.

"Just don't try bringing one into the Carlyle," Tina said.

"Are those places that say 'Thai massage' authentic?" Renee Wilde asked.

"I have *no* idea," TK said.

"So, man, how do you ask for happy ending in Thai?" Nestor asked.

"Try, *I want happy ending,*" TK said, "not that I am speaking from personal experience."

"Is happy ending what I think it is?" Garth wanted to know. He had inherited the Captain's role now that Sven was toast.

"Man, everybody knows 'happy ending,'" Nestor said, his speech noticeably slurred.

"I don't," Renee said. "Is it animal, vegetable, or mineral?"

"All of the above," Nestor said. "Imagine, instead of an actor, Garth's something real: a teamster driving a sixteen-wheeler down I-80 through the night in Nebraska, listening to Jesus radio, popping NoDoz, his back killing him, and suddenly there's a pink neon sign—not THAI MASSAGE. Just RUB DOWN. Five minutes later he's naked, blissed, as this pretty Asian woman slathers on oil and walks her magic fingers down his spine. And just as he's thinking it's over too soon, she asks, *Want happy ending?* That's not the moment to blurt: *Miss, is happy ending what I think it is? Is it authentic happy ending?* You say, *Oh, yeah!* And she says, *Happy ending, fifty dollar extra.* And man, there in the darkness of Nebraska you've learned the authentic price of happiness."

"I was going to suggest changing *EverAfter* to *Happy Ending,*" Renee Wilde said, "but now I'm afraid that would raise the wrong expectations in the audience."

"Wouldn't it be nice if life were that simple?" the Mogul asked. "If expectations were always fair and easily met? If all it took to find happiness was to know the right words for asking, and who to ask, and the going rate? Doesn't everyone want to know the magic words, and there's no shortage of religions, philosophies, gurus, psychologists, politicians all claiming to be able to tell us. Take Nixon and JFK in Tina's play: Nixon's telling America, *Here's my idea of happy ending*, and Kennedy is saying, *Well, here's mine*. Of course Tricky Dicky with his grizzled face was one morose-looking dude, and Jack Kennedy you knew was getting happy ending eight nights a week, so, bring on Camelot.

"Look at the talent in this one hotel room, the plays, films, music, books you people have produced. Isn't *authentic* Art—capital *A*—supposed to show us how to live happily ever after? I once went to a famous therapist, I won't drop his name or sticker-shock you with how much he thought his time was worth, and I told him: I've got everything a man could want—power, fame, fortune—I could go through ten reincarnations and not spend what I've made in this one lifetime. I've got a mansion in Santa Monica, a chateau in Provence, my own Pacific island, the best food and liquor, women JFK would have singing 'Happy Birthday, Mr. President' for him every day of the year. I can feel the envy when I enter a room, yet I'm not happy. First thing the shrink advises me to do is read this novel he thought would help me. I say, Doc, I know the author, I brought him to Hollywood and like most Artists, capital *A*, he was one of the most miserable fucks on the planet. I'm supposed to learn something about happiness from him? So the shrink immediately retreats to plan B, his Socratic fucking question: How do you define happiness? Like I'm going to pay in time and money to play semantic games, just so he doesn't have to admit he doesn't have a clue. And here I am, tonight, surrounded by artists, intellectuals, the New York literati—can any of you come up with a better answer?"

In the quiet, it was possible for the first time in the evening to hear the classical guitar music that had been playing in the background.

"Liam," the Mogul said, "you put this whole show together. Do you have an answer? Renee, you're a glamorous,
award-winning actress, how about you? TK, you've traveled
the world. Tina, you're witty enough to do stand-up comedy
on TV. Gil, we haven't had a chance to talk about passion yet,
but you're a hell of a writer. Anybody?"

The guests had formed a semicircle around the couch where
the Mogul sat alone with his ice bucket. They looked down into
their wine flutes, avoiding eye contact, sipping meditatively as
if mulling over his question, drinking as if that disguised the
embarrassing lack of response.

"I might," Gil said.

"And here I thought you of all people would shy away from
the subject," the Mogul said. "Because, you know, happiness
like passion can be a little *clichéd*. Let's hear it. An answer
could be worth the proverbial king's ransom."

"I can't tell you why you're unhappy," Gil said, "because
you aren't."

"Oh, I guarantee you that I am. I could produce some very
famous people willing to serve as witnesses."

"It's not a matter of what others say, is it?"

"Well, if it's simply my word against yours, who do you
think the jury will believe? Frankly, I'm going to be very disappointed if you're leading up to some semantic what-is-
happiness bullshit, because I'm talking naked, Gil. Gut level."

"Gut level, absolutely," Gil said. "What if I can prove you
are happy?"

Behind the carton-stacked coffee table, the Mogul leaned
forward on the couch as if not wanting to miss a word.

"I went to college on a track scholarship," Gil said.

"And you look like you've stayed in shape," the Mogul said.

"Thanks," Gil said. "My event was high hurdles. I put a
lot of practice into making my move out of the starting blocks
explosive. When you see hurdlers racing, knocking down

hurdles, it can look like a free-for-all, but it's actually a very controlled event. Every hurdler has the same number of strides between hurdles—usually three. That's about the distance between you and me. If you weren't expecting it, and why should you be, I could cross the room, hurdle the table, and before you could react jam these chopsticks in your eyes. And after you finished howling, and your long hospital stay was over and you were learning to feel your way with a white cane, you'd think back to tonight with the snow and the champagne and the smell of takeout that cooks sweating over spattering woks had ladled into cartons for a kid who probably can't speak English to bring us on his bike in the driving rain, and I bet you'd realize that you *were* happy. You just can't see it at this moment."

Except for Nestor's snoring, the room had gone dead silent. No one moved or spoke. The music had stopped.

"So, when do you say, 'Hey, just kidding'?" the Mogul finally asked.

The question released the tension in the room enough for Liam to rise—a little unsteadily—and say it was a great night but it was late and there was a rehearsal tomorrow, and grab his coat from the rack set up by the door. A mass exit of guests followed him out into the hall, grabbing their coats without pausing to put them on, and packed into the elevators.

The Mogul stayed on the couch.

Gil rode down in the elevator with Tina.

"I didn't know you ran track," she said.

"Artistic license, capital *A*," Gil said. "Third place in the state finals in high school was as far as I got."

"Where'd the chopsticks come from?"

"You know, until he said 'gut level' I was actually going to tell a story about a Chinese poet friend of mine who studied kung fu for thirty years at a dojo called the Sanctuary of Universal Peace. When he told me the dojo's name, I asked if he'd ever used kung fu to defend himself, and he said that wasn't why he studied. 'So, what are you after?' I asked, and he thought awhile, like he'd never considered it, then said: 'To be able to say thank you every minute.'"

"And 'thank you every minute' turned into chopsticks. Inspiration will do that," Tina said.

They stood beneath the hotel's gold-lit marquee while, over the wet hiss of traffic along Madison Avenue, the door-man whistled for cabs. When the wind gusted, snowflakes caught in Tina's hair and melted glittering in the marquee lights. She did look lovely. From the little she'd mentioned about her personal life—a runaway daughter now living at a drug rehab center, an ongoing divorce from a man she de-scribed as "a decent guy who still adores me"—Gil knew she was going through a difficult time. He wondered how she was managing to work as well as she was. He had told her at Papaya King, months ago, that her piece, "Dick Jokes," and Nestor's musical score were the only really solid things about *EverAfter*.

"When I get home, just before I pass out, I'm going to think about tonight and laugh myself to sleep," Tina said. "Hopefully it will keep off the spins."

"Don't forget to picture Sven doing the crotch-grab while singing 'Slow Boat to China,'" Gil said.

"That's too ha-ha sad," Tina said. "But then, maybe he'll have the final revenge after he incorporates some crotch work to rave reviews the next time he plays *Lear*."

A cab pulled up. "I won't bother to ask if you want to share a ride," she said.

"I'm going to walk in the park."

She kissed him good night lightly on the cheek and he closed the door of the cab after her and stood watching her pull away. The cab started and stopped. Tina rolled down the window. "Gil, one more thing. If I were you, I wouldn't be planning to give up my teaching job just yet."

She gave a wave and he waved back.

The cab started and stopped again. Tina rolled down the window. "One more one more thing," she called. "If you want to say it every minute, you have to start with one minute. Thank you."

Fiction

Through a rift in the mist, a moon the shade of water-stained silk. A night to begin, to begin again. Someone whistling a tune impossible to find on a piano, an elusive melody that resides, perhaps, in the spaces between the keys where there once seemed to be only silence. He wants to tell her a story without telling a story. One in which the silence between words is necessary in order to make audible the faint whistle of her breath as he enters her.

Or rather than a sound, or even the absence of sound, the story might at first be no more than a scent: a measure of the time spent folded in a cedar drawer that's detectable on a silk camisole. For illumination, other than the moonlight (now momentarily clouded), it's lit by the flicker of an almond candle against a bureau mirror that imprisons light as a jewel does a flame.

The amber pendant she wears tonight, for instance, a gem he's begun to suspect has not yet fossilized into form. It's still flowing, imperceptibly, like a bead of clover honey between the cleft of her breasts. Each night it changes shape—one night an ellipse, on another a tear, or a globe, lunette or gibbous, as if it moved through phases like an amber moon. Each morning it has captured something new—moss, lichen, pine needles. On one morning he notices a wasp, no doubt extinct, from the time before the invention of language, preserved in such perfect detail that it looks dangerous, still able to sting. On another morning the faint hum of a trapped bee, and on another, a glint of prehistoric sun along a captured mayfly's wings. Where she grazes down his body and her honey-colored hair and the dangling pendant brush across his skin, he can feel the warmth of sunlight trapped in amber. Or is that simply body heat?

The story could have begun with the faint hum of a bee. Is something so arbitrary as a beginning even required? He wants to tell her a story without a beginning, a story that goes through phases like a moon, the telling of which requires the proper spacing of a night sky between each phase.

Imagine the words strung out across the darkness, and the silent spaces between them as the emptiness that binds a snowfall together, or turns a hundred starlings rising from a wire into a single flock, or countless stars into a constellation. A story of stars, or starlings. A story of falling snow. Of words swept up and bound like whirling leaves. Or, after the leaves have settled, a story of mist.

What chance did words have beside the distraction of her body? He wanted to go where language couldn't take him, wanted to listen to her breath break speechless from its cage of parentheses, to travel wordlessly across her skin like that flush that would spread between her nape and breasts. What was that stretch of body called? He wanted a narrative that led to all the places where her body was still undiscovered, unclaimed, unnamed.

Fiction—"the lie through which we tell the truth," as Camus famously said—was at once too paradoxical and yet not mysterious enough. A simpler kind of lie was needed, one that didn't turn back upon itself and violate the very meaning of lying. A lie without dénouement, epiphany, or escape into revelation, a lie that remained elusive. The only lie he needed was the one that would permit them to keep on going as they had.

It wasn't the shock of recognition, but the shock of what had become unrecognizable that he now listened for. It wasn't a suspension of disbelief, but a suspension of common sense that loving her required.

Might unconnected details be enough, arranged and re-arranged in any order? A scent of cedar released by body heat from a water-stained camisole. The grain of the hair she'd shaved from her underarms, detectable against his lips. The fading mark of a pendant impressed on her skin by the weight of his body. (If not a resinous trail left by a bead of amber along her breasts, then it's her sweat that's honey.) Another night upon which this might end—might end again, for good this time: someone out on the misty street, whistling a melody impossible to re-create . . .

I wanted to tell you a story without telling the story.

Inland Sea

Horizon, a clothesline strung between crabapples. The forgotten dress, that far away, bleached invisible by a succession of summer days until a thunderstorm drenches it blue again, as it is now, and despite the distance, the foam of raindrops at its hem sparkles just before the wind lifts it into a wave that breaks against the man framed in a farmhouse doorway.

Pink Ocean

I dreamed in negative exposure of a room where night and light sound nothing alike and so are not balanced in opposition. A room expelled from a children's story because its clock won't go ticktock and there's no hat for a cat or a spoon to reflect the moon. The only illumination a levitating dress, a handkerchief bidding farewell from a steamer, the gossamer curtain suspended on the thermal of a hissing radiator.

Beyond the curtain, a window open on to outer space.

Beneath stars like those that Dante sees again—*a rive-der le stelle*—when he emerges from the Inferno, she led the blindered horses of childhood from a burning barn and woke to a momentary scent of cigar smoke.

I've heard it defies the conventions of dreams to touch a ghost animal. Yet, when for one last time I was allowed to gather that beautiful contradiction called cat—twelve silky pounds of wildness—into my arms, I didn't want to let him go. It was only a moment before I awoke from his familiar warmth, so maybe the restriction against touching ghost animals *was* enforced, only not quickly enough.

Freud said dreams are wishes. Once, I cut off my mother's hands.

Whatever else dreams may be, they're a kind of recollection. It doesn't matter that mostly they're forgotten, vanished like those theoretical elements conceived in a cyclotron whose existence is measured in nanoseconds.

Whatever else dreams may be, she said, they make for conversation.

We were trading dreams in a Jeep Cherokee that smelled of hay. Ours were the only cars left in a parking lot that was vanishing in a snowfall. When the neon sign blinked out, the flakes went from pink to white. We'd met for a drink at a restaurant fittingly called, given the snow, the Lodge. It's been gone for years, but sometimes I'll still see it when I drive by if I ignore the seedy antique shop in its place. A mutual friend had mentioned to her that I might be of help in suggesting journals to which she could submit her poems. I was teaching "Your Life as Poetry"—not a title I'd chosen—at a community center for seniors. My students all wanted to know what ever became of rhyme. She taught riding to the blind, the friend told me, and lived on a horse farm. I don't know what I expected—cowboy poetry, greeting-card verse about horses running free? At the very least her poems were the work of a sophisticated reader, written in a current style: free verse in which the poet addressed herself as *you*. Their subject, besides the *you*, was abandoned barns—a sequence that explored old barns as photographers do, but the barns in her poems could have only been constructed out of language. Barns the horizon showed through, composed more of slatted light, motes, and cobwebs than from warped siding, their tattered roofs askew beneath the frown of crows; barns like beds unmade by tornadoes, weather vanes still dizzy; washed-up barns, driftwood gray, flotsamed with rusted, mysterious tools; barns shingled in license plates, their only history a progression of dates—different colors, same state: decay. Unhinged doors gaping shadow and must, recurring hints about divorce and childlessness—a few would make it to the pages of literary magazines.

Instead of real drinks, we both ordered tea, which at the Lodge was hot water and Lipton's with a wedge of lemon. And here we were, past midnight, in the front seat of her Jeep, a woolen horse blanket over our laps. I was telling her how I once woke with only a phrase in mind: *primary play at binary speed*.

Meaning what? she asked.

Maybe the motto for the way I've lived my life, or should be living it.

Maybe you dreamed your epitaph, she said.

Barns in which a conflagration lurked, but where? Not amid the stalls or in the tack room. A faint whiff of cigar, more threatening than an ax. Barns with rooms so secret not even their rodents knew where the keys were hidden.

In a hidden room, a room expelled from a children's story, the child who was myself wakes sweaty, needing to pee. A psychopath stalks the flat. His bare feet creak unevenly beneath the heft of the ax on his shoulder as he pads down the long hallway toward my room. Some nights his rolling eyes can see in the dark. On others he gropes along the walls, more terrifying still as he'll have to find me by touch.

Three a.m. in the soul. The clock ticks but won't tock. No rhyme or reason, my mother used to say.

Meaning what? you ask.

Meaning my seniors miss more than rhyme's mnemonic power. In *Remembrance of Things Past*, Proust remarks that the tyranny of rhyme forces poets into their greatest lines. Senior citizens are pro-tyrant. Rhyme is tactile to them. When absent it seems there's no other way to get from cat to hat, from spoon to moon.

From clock, ticktock, to the mad, homemade puppet of a

sock named Frère Jacques with the brain of a rock, which could blackjack the psychopath whose fingertips just brushed my face.

Shhh, it's only the touch of the curtain rising on the thermal of steam heat, a levitating dress fluttering farewell. Sometimes the inanimate comes alive not to terrify but to console.

Shhh, the smell of the inferno raging at the tip of a cigar may simply be the friction between the lilac tree beside your open window and the wild leeks that spike in spring from the pasture where a horse barn resonates in the wind, amplifying the twang of barbed wire and hum of electric fence.

A barn that a country song would rhyme with empty arms.

What's your favorite rhyme ever? Shakespeare, Emily Dickinson, Yeats, Cole Porter . . . It's a one-way question, she said, so please don't answer, what's yours?

I guess the best questions are impossible to answer, I said.

Give me the impossible.

Before we slip into unconsciousness / I'd like to have another kiss.

At the Monet exhibition a little girl reaches out and cries, "Look! Pink ocean!"

A guard rushes over and says, "No one is allowed to touch the paintings, and no photographs."

The *You* of the barn poems and I are at the exhibition. We leave Monet behind and browse through rooms of martyrs, Virgins, bloody Christs, and then along a corridor of gracefully muscled statues whose mutilation has over eons come to look as if it were forecast in the original conception. Beheaded torsos that remain beautiful, shoulders no less perfect for their amputated arms, breasts still those of Venus despite chips where there presumably were nipples. Posed beside an uncastrated Apollo, she hands me the disposable camera she'd concealed in her purse.

Quick! she says. Before the guard comes, take one of me kissing the cock of a god.

You must change your life, I tell her.

Says who?

At what degree of dusk and dilapidation does a barn / pass from the temporal of architecture / to the eternal of sculpture? one of her poems asks before concluding: *Sculpture is made to touch / careful, Love, splinters.*

Ever notice the eyes that stare from the word *look*? she asks. Is that an accident or a reminder of how close language once was to pictures? Clay tablets, hieroglyphs, calligraphy—before computers, the act of writing, whether carving with a pen or hammering with a typewriter, was physical, but now who except the blind touch language? Riding a horse blind is one thing, but reading blind—imagine, running your fingertips across a page like touching the unseen body of a lover, and suddenly: Look! Pink ocean!

Or a barn raised from parachuting dandelion seeds that as kids we called money-stealers, a levitating barn shimmering like the dragonflies we called ear-stingers, a ghost barn erected from swamp mist, raftered with fireflies.

That ghost cat and I were young together. Even asleep I can sense the curtain lifting. I can't dream him without remembering being happy. Beyond the curtain, on an island, I snorkel along our dock hoping for a fish for supper and the cat follows down the dock. Sometimes I'd spear a small fish for him, a squirrelfish or a sergeant major, toss it up, and he'd carry it in his mouth so the herons didn't get it. A dream is a kind of remembering. The curtain waves farewell. As I gun my old Triumph into a curve of highway beside the sea, my infant son, riding on my lap like a baguette, is flung by the momentum of my maniacal driving into the turquoise water and floats off like driftwood. Inconsolable, I kneel weeping beside my motorcycle, and a passerby stops to ask the trouble and I say I've lost my little son, and the passerby, trying to be kind, says, Don't worry, you can have another.

But that was the one I wanted, I tell her.

The psycho has entered the barn, spooked the horses, violated the secret rooms. Eyeing her silhouette on the shade, he's caressed himself on a bale of sweet hay, and afterward lights a cigar. Where is he from, what brings him here repeatedly?— some Depression-era specter, a hobo cursed to travel endless freights, some tramp on the lam who has leaped from the train whose distant whistle I could hear from your window, Love, when I woke to you beside me moaning in your sleep at three a.m. To your familiar warmth; I didn't want to let go. *Shhh.* It's only a train plowing through fields as if pulling its own wreckage, approaching in the dark the unmarked crossing of the country road I'd jounce over on the way to your farm. Owls and swallows, a barn of rhyming birds audible at the end of a dirt road. A red barn on the coast of a pink pond. Lilacs. A pasture where *look* lowers its lids and becomes the scent of wild leeks.

Acknowledgments

Thank you to the editors of the magazines in which these stories were first published, in slightly different form:

Alaska Quarterly Review: "Current," "Brisket"
Boulevard: "Fridge"
Colorado Review: "Ransom," "Between," "Wash"
Connecticut Review: "Fedora"
Cottonwood: "Dark Ages" (first published as "Among Nymphs")
Epoch: "Bruise," "Coat"
Herman Review: "The Kiss"
Image: "Flies"
Indiana Review: "Voyeur of Rain"
Joe: "Fantasy"
Manoa: "Confession," "The Samaritan" (first published as "The Girl Downstairs")
McSweeney's: "Happy Ending"
Michigan Quarterly Review: "The Story of Mist"
Monkey Business: "Naked"
New Letters: "Transaction"
O, The Oprah Magazine: "Vista di Mare"
Oxford Magazine: "Alms"
Playboy: "Tea Ceremony"
Ploughshares: "Misterioso," "A Confluence of Doors," "Ant," "Swing"

Poetry: "Pink Ocean"
Quarterly West: "Aria"
Rattapallax: "Goodwill"
Telescope: "Midwife"
The Idaho Review: "Ice"
The Iowa Review: "Here Comes the Sun"
The Literarian: "Inland Sea"
The Ohio Review: "Transients Welcome"
The Pequod: "Fingerprints"
The Seattle Review: "Belly Button"
The Southern Review: "The Question," "Ordinary Nudes"
The Washington Post Magazine: "Córdoba"
Tin House: "The Start of Something," "Arf," "Fiction"
Transatlantic Review: "Ravenswood" (first published as "The Conductor, the Nun, the Streetcar")
TriQuarterly: "I Never Told This to Anyone," "Flu"
X, A Journal of the Arts: "Hometown"
Witness: "Drive"

Thanks also to the editors of the following magazines in which later versions of some of these stories were published: *After Hours*; *Dimensional Lines*; *Flash*; *Jelly Bucket*; *Mirabella*; *Oak Bend Review*; *Skywriting*; *SmokeLong Quarterly*; *The Mac-Guffin*; *Memphis State Review*; *The Nervous Breakdown*; *Water-Stone Review*.

And thank you to the editors of the following anthologies in which some of these pieces appeared: *An Anthology of Very Short Fiction*, Flatmancrooked Press; *Bestial Noise*, Tin House Books; *Blue Cathedral*, Red Hen Press; *Field Guide to Writing Flash Fiction*, Rose Metal Press; *Flash Fiction Funny*, Blue Light Press; *Flash Fiction International*, Norton; *Hint Fiction*, Norton; *Just Good Reading from the Pages of "The Critic,"* Thomas More Press; *Micro*, White Pine Press; *Micro Fiction*,

Norton; *PP/FF*, Starcherone Books; *Shorts*, Norton; *Sudden Flash Youth*, Persea Books; *The Party Train*, White Pine Press; *The Southern California Anthology*, the University of Southern California Master of Professional Writing Program; *The Wedding Cake in the Middle of the Road*, Norton.

A special thanks to Motoyuki Shibata and to Philippe Biget for their translations of some of these pieces into Japanese and French; to Susan Stamberg and NPR's *Weekend Edition*, who first commissioned and broadcast "I Never Told This to Anyone"; and to Judith Kitchen and Stan Rubin, founders of the State Street Press, Brockport, New York, which in 1993 published a twenty-eight-page chapbook titled *The Story of Mist*, in which several of these pieces, in earlier versions, appeared.

This book was finished and reworked during time afforded by a fellowship from the MacArthur Foundation.